The
Secret
of my
Seduction

❧ THE SCANDALS SERIES ❧

Books by Caroline Linden

WHEN THE MARQUESS WAS MINE
AN EARL LIKE YOU
MY ONCE AND FUTURE DUKE
AT THE CHRISTMAS WEDDING
THE SECRET OF MY SEDUCTION
DRESSED TO KISS
SIX DEGREES OF SCANDAL
A STUDY IN SCANDAL
LOVE IN THE TIME OF SCANDAL
ALL'S FAIR IN LOVE AND SCANDAL
IT TAKES A SCANDAL
LOVE AND OTHER SCANDALS
AT THE DUKE'S WEDDING
THE WAY TO A DUKE'S HEART
BLAME IT ON BATH
ONE NIGHT IN LONDON
I LOVE THE EARL
YOU ONLY LOVE ONCE
FOR YOUR ARMS ONLY
A VIEW TO A KISS
A RAKE'S GUIDE TO SEDUCTION
WHAT A ROGUE DESIRES
WHAT A GENTLEMAN WANTS
WHAT A WOMAN NEEDS

AT THE BILLIONAIRE'S WEDDING

The
Secret
of my
Seduction

⤙ THE SCANDALS SERIES ⤚

CAROLINE

LINDEN

Copyright © 2017 P.F. Belsley

Cover design: Carrie Divine/Seductive Designs
Image: Novelstock
Image: Olga Saksa/Depositphotos

ISBN: 0-9971494-4-2
ISBN-13: 978-0-9971494-4-9

Printed in the USA

To every reader who's ever written a fan letter to an author.
You make our day every time.

Chapter One

1823
London

Despite her looks, Bathsheba Crawford had never been shy.

Most people thought she would be. She was no beauty, with a round face and plain features, her hair an ordinary shade of brown. She could not sing, had never learned to play an instrument, and didn't speak a word of French. There was nothing distinguishing about her, really.

But her mind worked quite well, thank you very much. With no expectation of getting by on her looks or charm, Bathsheba had learned to use the talents she did have: an unmatched memory, a sharp, practical intelligence, and the ability to listen more than she spoke. She also learned to pursue what she wanted, because nothing was freely given to young women of unremarkable looks whom everyone believed quiet and withdrawn.

That had seen her through hardship and adversity when her parents died of consumption and their family printing business failed. When her brother Daniel came home from war missing part of his arm, unable to work. When they came within a hair's breadth of losing everything. It also

1

drove her to seize opportunities when they arose: taking a chance on printing a scandalous story called *Fifty Ways to Sin* on the old printing press sitting idle in their scullery, which succeeded beyond all their dreams, and then daring to write her own wicked novels, even if anonymously.

She might still be a plain little mouse of a woman, but she was a successful one. Her *Tales of Lady X*, about the romantic follies of a daring adventuress, sold very well. Whenever she caught the faintly pitying glances people sent her way ("The poor dear, so plain and quiet, no wonder she's a spinster…") or the openly surprised glances when she said something sensible ("Oh, good heavens; Miss Crawford, we didn't notice you…"), a fierce satisfaction burned like a small sun in her breast. She *was* someone, even if none of them knew it.

She reminded herself of all this as she approached the *London Intelligencer*, a gossip newspaper. She was here on business, after all, and Liam MacGregor had long recognized her head for business. He was the owner and publisher of the *Intelligencer*, a strong-minded, ambitious Scot with a taste for risk. He'd become their partner in the final frantic days of printing *Fifty Ways to Sin*. If Bathsheba knew anything about Liam, it was that he never said no to a profitable proposal.

She went through the *Intelligencer*'s ramshackle offices and knocked on Liam's door. A muffled shout was all the welcome she received; he didn't even look up from his task when she came in and closed the door.

Bathsheba was undaunted. "I have a proposal," she announced. "A business matter."

Liam's eyebrow arched, although he didn't raise his head from the newspaper copy he was reading. "What is it?"

So direct. She admired that about him. Bathsheba was

neither delicate nor missish, but now that she'd come to the point, she'd rather only have to say it once. "*Tales of Lady X* are selling well—"

Liam flashed a fierce grin at her before dropping his gaze back to the copy. Nothing pleased him more than success, and her novels were one of his biggest. Bathsheba appreciated that about him; he hadn't quailed or scoffed when she brought him her manuscript. Instead he spotted its potential at once, to the benefit of both their purses.

Buoyed, she took a seat and went on. "*Quite* well. But I believe the tales could be even better. Lady Constance and *Fifty Ways to Sin* proved there is a real hunger for stories of genuine passion, and of course I want to find every way to improve. And after much thought, I think there is one thing which would notably better my stories."

Finally his head came up. "Oh?"

She gripped her hands a little tighter together, keeping her eyes locked on his. Given what she was about to suggest, she ought to be able to do that, at the very least. It wasn't a hardship to look at him. Liam was handsome in a sharp, bold way, with broad, high cheekbones and a straight nose over a rather sensual mouth. If anything, his eyes were the most unsettling part of him; they were gray, and when he was annoyed or angry, they could pale to an almost unearthly color. Now they were fixed on her, unflinching and bright beneath the too-long waves of his dark hair.

"I lack—" She stopped, the words suddenly thick and wooly in her mouth. "I need—"

"Run out of ideas?" he asked.

She shook her head. Not ideas. Bathsheba had plenty of ideas for her books. It was something more practical that she lacked, and it was beginning to affect her work.

"What?" His forehead creased. "Don't tell me you've written too indiscreetly about a past lover and he's going to make trouble."

"Don't be stupid," she snapped. "Of course not." It was insulting that he would think her that careless.

His expression cleared of irritation, but the interest remained. "Then what is it? Do you need funds advanced?"

He should know she didn't. Her share of the profits had accumulated to a tidy sum. She pressed her hands flat on her knees. "No. I lack deeper knowledge of my subject."

It took him a moment, but Liam realized her meaning. "No," he said in sly disbelief. "Don't tell me you're a—"

"No, but near enough," she said impatiently. She wasn't a virgin, but her carnal experience was limited, and—to put it mildly—uninspiring.

"Then how have you written—?"

"From *Fifty Ways to Sin*." She glared at him, too smug and handsome with his cravat loosened and the sun gleaming on his hair. It wasn't her fault she didn't have a large number of past lovers. If anything, the *Fifty Ways to Sin* stories had made her very sorry for that fact, as they had opened her eyes to the existence of a world of sensual pleasure she'd barely imagined. Who wouldn't want to experience the bliss described in them?

But the fact remained that she had not; her quiet, mousy appearance was to blame, no doubt.

"And from gossip," she went on. "It's not hard to overhear the most scandalous and depraved things, as you well know. A woman can learn quite a bit." All the gossip Bathsheba had heard indicated those pleasures were no fiction, although neither were they commonplace.

He laughed. "I do know! I just never thought—" He stopped short and cleared his throat. "Well, do what you

4

must."

Bathsheba kept her composure by the narrowest of margins. Liam could be cold and calculating, and he didn't waste time on platitudes or trivial conversation. Generally she admired that. "I plan to. Since it's as much to your benefit as it is to mine that the . . . er . . . experience be as thorough and as inspirational as possible, I propose that you assist."

For the first time she could ever recall, Liam's face went blank, then flushed a girlish shade of pink. He didn't even sputter or protest, just stared at her in disbelief.

Bathsheba raised her brows, pleased to have silenced him for once. "It's for the benefit of our mutual business endeavor."

"You want *me*—?" Liam's eyes narrowed. "What sort of idiot do you think I am?"

She frowned. "Not an idiot. I'm not asking you to fall in love with me or even engage in a prolonged affair. Three or four times ought to be sufficient. Think of it as a research inquiry."

"I am not a scientific experiment!"

"Neither am I," she said coolly. "But I know you've got quite a reputation with the ladies—or so says the gossip—and I'd rather learn from the best."

His face was still flushed. "How dare you gossip about me."

"You don't mind if I listen to every sort of tawdry tale about everyone else in society, but your name is beyond the pale?" She gave him a reproving look in spite of herself. "You encouraged me to listen. It's hard to stop when a familiar name comes up."

"You could if you tried," he snarled, shoving back from his desk and bounding to his feet. "What the blazes would your brother say if he knew what you just asked me to do?"

"Good heavens, why would you tell him?" she exclaimed. Daniel didn't even know Liam published her books. That had been her bargain with Liam: he must keep her identity secret at all costs, from Daniel and from the rest of the world. "It's none of his concern. I'm twenty-nine years old, not a little girl Danny must protect."

"'Tis a bloody stupid idea," he snapped, sounding more Scottish than ever. "Put it from your head."

Bathsheba sighed. She'd braced herself for this reply, but it was still disappointing. "I take it that means no. Very well." She got to her feet, then hesitated. "I trust you'll be kind enough not to tell anyone about this."

"Of course not—" He glared at her. "What are you going to do now?"

"Find someone else, obviously."

"Don't you dare!" In three strides he was across the room, barring the door before she could march through it. "Where did this lunatic idea come from?"

He had wedged himself between her and the door. Bathsheba had never been so close to him—nor to any man who exerted this sort of pull on her—but she refused to back away. He was only half a head taller than she, but her pulse skipped a beat as she looked up at him.

"The usual urges, Liam," she said, quietly but firmly. "How can I write about lovemaking all day and not wonder if I'm describing it accurately?" Not to mention lying awake at nights perishing of curiosity about the heights of bliss one could achieve, with the right lover.

He looked like a storm cloud, dark hair curling wildly against his loose collar and his eyes turbulent. "Who would you ask?"

"I've spent enough time among the rakes and

scoundrels of London to know it won't be impossible to find one willing to toss up my skirts. I had hoped to avoid it being a stranger, but—"

"Sit down," he growled. He jerked his head toward the chair she had just vacated.

Surprised, Bathsheba sat down.

Watching her closely, Liam paced the confines of his cluttered office. He combed one hand through his hair, mussing it even more, and Bathsheba's stomach contracted involuntarily. No, she didn't want it to be a stranger . . . She wanted to learn passion from a handsome, slightly dangerous man, and Liam fit the bill in every particular. The fact that he knew her, respected her, treated her as an equal for good and for ill, just made it even more logical that she should ask him.

The fact that she found him wildly, irrationally attractive ought not to figure into it, except as a private measure of delight for her. At first she had feared that was a fatal weakness in her plan, as his answer would matter far more to her than it should, but she had persuaded herself it was worth the risk. What was the harm in giving in to her secret infatuation?

But who knew he would turn into a stuffy prude at the first mention of a casual affair? Bathsheba spent her evenings haunting the edges of society. Everything she'd overheard indicated that rakes wanted precisely that: not love, not attachment, nothing but a few passionate nights in bed.

Of course, she'd also heard that rakes enjoyed the chase, the thrill of pursuing a reluctant woman, and she'd just scotched any prospect of that. But when she thought of how long it would take to entice Liam into wanting her, then pursuing her, pretending reluctance, before finally succumbing . . . Who had time for that? She wanted to know *now*.

Finally Liam stopped pacing. "Why do you think you need more experience?" A bit of the flush returned as he spoke the last word. "*Lady X* sells quite well; just keep on doing what you're doing."

"It's getting stale," she tried to say, but he slashed one hand.

"Bollocks. Just write more of the same. People love it."

"It's boring *me*."

His eyebrows shot up. "Boring! You wrote of an encounter in Hyde Park in the last installment."

Her mouth turned down. All the excitement of that chapter had revolved around the prospect of Lady X getting caught with her lover making love in a stand of trees not far from the carriageway. Bathsheba understood all about the sick terror of getting caught doing something illicit and risking being exposed and humiliated. What she didn't know, at least not well enough, was the craving for another person that would drive someone to risk everything for those few minutes of rapture. "I can't keep writing stories where the sole source of tension is the location of the encounter."

"Why not?"

She threw her arms wide. "Where else would you have me set a story? In the British Museum? Onstage in Drury Lane? If you suggest a Royal Drawing Room, I shall slap your face."

He waved one hand irritably. "Of course I would never suggest that. You've never been—"

Blessedly, he stopped before finishing it, but Bathsheba knew what he meant. She'd never been anywhere half so elegant and wouldn't have the first idea how to describe a

Drawing Room reception at St. James's Palace. Since it was true, she didn't dwell on the faint sting of the words, but seized on the fact that he'd proved her point. "Exactly! I've never been to the Court of St. James, so I couldn't possibly write sensibly about it. The same is true of this other matter. However, while I am highly unlikely ever to receive an invitation to St. James's, I bloody well can find a man to take me to bed."

For some reason, whenever she swore, Liam took her more seriously. He did this time as well, dropping into the chair beside her. "I just don't think it's necessary," he argued.

Bathsheba could see the fight had gone out of him. "That's why you're the publisher and I'm the author," she said firmly. "It's not your place to have good story ideas. Your job is to take full advantage of my good ideas. Don't worry, Liam. I promise to be discreet and not betray any hint of the truth in a tale."

He stared at her for a long moment. "Why me?"

Again Bathsheba's stomach clenched involuntarily. Was he relenting? Something hot and exhilarating bubbled up in her chest for a moment before she forced it down. "Because it's for our joint business," she said aloud, reminding herself as much as telling him. "Because I know you and believe you would be discreet—it not being in either of our interests to reveal it. And because the rumors about you are impressive—" She stopped and had to look away as his gaze grew faintly amused. "Are you reconsidering?"

He leaned forward. "Bathsheba," he said in the soft Scottish drawl that always caused unwarranted tremors to shiver through her. "Are you trying to seduce me?"

Yes. She would die before saying it out loud. "Would it

9

be faster to try to hire you?"

Liam laughed. "You couldn't afford me, love." He sat back and ran a speculative gaze over her. Bathsheba tried not to feel the way her nipples hardened as his gray eyes lingered on her bosom. If any other man had ever looked at her breasts that way, she couldn't recall it. "But for business . . . You know the way to my heart. I'll do it."

She blinked. "Lovely."

"Where do you propose to conduct this reseach?"

"Er." She hadn't worked that out. In fact, she was only now realizing that she hadn't truly expected him to agree. "I'll let you know."

But he'd seen. His eyes now gleaming with satisfaction, Liam surged out of his chair. "No, no, I'll arrange it." He gave her a look, the hint of a smirk curling his mouth. "Based on my greater expertise in the subject."

Bathsheba's wits had been somewhat scrambled by the lightning-fast change in his attitude. "Lovely," she repeated in the same blank tone.

Liam crossed his arms over his chest—rather a broad chest, now that she looked at it anew—and smiled. Not a smirk, not a ruthless twist of his lips, but a sensual expression that hinted of wickedness beyond her wildest imagination. Which was what she had wanted, but perhaps not quite what she had expected. "It will be, love," he promised. "It will be."

Chapter Two

"**W**hat scandals are you exploiting these days?" Angus lined up his cue and squinted at his ball.

Liam sipped his whisky. "As many as I can find."

His brother grunted and made his shot, scoring a cannon as his ball hit two others. "It's not like you to keep something from Mother."

"Mother hears at least as much as I print in the paper."

Angus cocked his head and made another shot, sending Liam's ball across the green baize and almost potting it in the corner pocket. Almost, but not quite.

Liam grinned vindictively. He and his brother played cutthroat billiards rules; any foul wiped out all a player's points in a round. It was a tradition of theirs after Sunday dinner at their mother's home. At times Liam suspected she'd bought this billiard table strictly to lure them here. Thin-lipped, Angus stepped aside. Liam did not intend to yield the table again. He set down his glass and reached for his cue.

"I can tell you've got something." Angus picked up the piece of lambswool they used to clean the cues. In a competitive fit, Angus had had a cue made to his personal specifications. Liam had mocked him for that, even though he'd secretly had a custom stick made as well, an exact match in appearance for those in his mother's cabinet, and substituted it for one of the ordinary cues. Since Angus only used his personal cue, and no one else played billiards on Mrs. MacGregor's table, the replacement had gone unnoticed.

Now Liam hefted his perfectly weighted cue stick and surveyed the table. He did so enjoy ruining his older brother at billiards. "Two guineas a round, was it?"

"One," said Angus curtly. "Wake me if you ever make a shot."

"Go ahead and close your eyes," murmured Liam, calculating the angles and lining up his plan of attack. "Perhaps then you won't bawl like a child when I trounce you."

"Who's the new woman writing for you?" Angus asked just as he made his shot.

Liam swore at him. "That's cheating."

"Just idle conversation," protested his brother with a gleam of false sincerity in his eyes. "Mother's been dying to know."

He glared. By some miracle, his shot hadn't gone too far awry and he'd scored a point. Not the two points he had lined up, but it meant he kept control of the table. "It's not really her concern, is it?"

While his father had fretted over Liam's choice of profession, his mother had been entranced; now her son was privy to all the choicest gossip in London. Mrs. MacGregor's favorite stories were about the Royal family, but anyone with a title was almost as good. The scandalous doings of her betters consumed Mrs. MacGregor's attention.

Liam knew his mother read *Tales of Lady X*; he brought her every installment, along with copies of the *Intelligencer*'s scandal and gossip columns. She adored both, and never stopped trying to guess the identities of both authors. Fortunately Liam was used to fending off his mother.

"No," said Angus, drawing out the word, "but it's so intriguing that you won't tell her, even after she vowed to be bound by secrecy."

"We both know that would last as long as it took for her to call for the carriage and drive to Mrs. Lachlan's home." Liam recognized the questioning as a ploy to distract him again, and consequently said nothing else until he'd made his next shot, and the one after, clearing the table and winning the round.

Grim-faced, Angus slapped a guinea on the green felt. Now they both had to play around it, and whoever racked up the most points in an hour collected all the guineas on the table. At this point, Liam didn't even remember the proper rules of billiards, but he didn't care. The times he walked home, pockets heavy with Angus's guineas, were celebratory occasions.

"You know," Angus said casually, cleaning his cue and preparing for the next round, "some fellows mutter against you for hiring women."

"Envious bastards," was Liam's languid reply.

"And women who write such scandalous things, too," Angus went on. "Ladies cavorting with all manner of men!"

Liam gave a bark of laughter. Either Angus had started reading *Lady X*, or he'd been listening too much to their mother. "As if they would turn down a woman who wanted to seduce them! Men haven't any high ground to stand on when it comes to seduction." He poured more whisky for both of them. "You'll have to trust me on that last bit, of course."

Angus cursed and took his shot. To Liam's private

disgust, he scored another point. "What the bloody hell does that mean?"

"Merely that I doubt women stroll into the bank and try to seduce you." Liam spoke soothingly, as if he were gently explaining some gross injustice Angus had no choice but to tolerate. No doubt he did; while Liam had got their mother's fair skin and wavy dark hair, Angus was nearly identical to their father, ginger-haired, red-faced, and built like a bull.

His brother raised his eyebrows. "And do they stroll into the newspaper offices and offer to raise their skirts for you?"

In spite of himself, a small smile curved Liam's lips. "On occasion."

Angus started. "No!"

"Are you ceding the table?"

"No!" Angus lined up a shot, then abandoned the pose. "Not really. You're having fun with me, eh?"

Liam sipped his drink and said nothing.

Angus threw down his cue. "By God, you bloody liar! You can't mean it. What woman—? Why? And when the bloody hell—?" He shook his head in disgust. "I'm done." He turned and stomped toward the door.

"Wait," said Liam in mock disgust. "Such a poor sport you are, to leave before the game is done."

His brother stopped in the doorway. "Admit you were lying about women offering to raise their skirts for you."

"Can't."

"Won't," scoffed Angus.

Liam raised his glass and cocked his head in admonishment. "Can't, because it's true."

"Who?"

"I'll tell you who when hell freezes," Liam shot back.

"What sort of gentleman do you take me for?"

For a long moment Angus glared at him. "Is she a fetching lass?"

He sipped his whisky and pondered it. Was Bathsheba fetching? Because she was the only woman who'd ever offered him such a proposition. She wasn't a beauty in the usual sense, but there *was* something about her. He knew she could be quiet and unremarkable when she wanted to be, but she had a spine of steel and a mind to match. When she set her sights on something, woe betide the fellow who tried to deny her.

How ironic that she'd set her sights on him. A faint smile curved his mouth at the memory of her blunt request. "She's not a conventional beauty," he finally said, "but she's arresting all the same."

Reluctantly Angus came back to the table. "Why you?"

Liam bared his teeth in a wide smile. "My devilish charm and irresistible masculinity."

His brother roared with laughter. "Money! She wants to snare you in the parson's noose, now that your gossip rag is profitable."

It was profitable thanks to Bathsheba. Her *Tales of Lady X* outsold the newspaper. Even he hadn't predicted that much appeal in them. But the result was that Bathsheba was making as much as he was, since they split the profits evenly. She wrote them, he published them . . . and he kept her identity an absolute secret. Her own brother didn't know she was the author, even though Daniel Crawford did business with Liam at times.

So he simply shrugged at his brother's goading comment. "Perhaps."

That seemed to appease Angus. He gave a patronizing smile and held out his glass. "Pour us another, would you?

I can't let you walk away with my money."

An hour later Liam did walk away, eight guineas richer. Angus had made a variety of halfhearted threats and curses, which always buoyed Liam's mood even more than winning his brother's money. Angus departed after muttering once more that Liam was a damned liar, claiming women were chasing him. Liam had held his tongue and made a show of collecting the guineas, going so far as to whistle a jaunty tune as he did so. That, he knew, would bother Angus more than any quarrel ever could.

Still . . . He didn't like that Bathsheba was an object of gossip, even if no one knew her name. For a moment he considered reneging on his agreement, but only for a moment. The last thing he wanted to do was let her venture out into London in search of a man to ravish her. He freely admitted it had never occurred to him to seduce her, but now that she'd planted the thought, damned if it hadn't taken root and pervaded his brain.

And she wanted it to be passionate and wild, to throw her world off kilter and leave her dazzled. What exactly did she expect, he wondered. Liam knew she haunted the public assemblies and pleasure gardens, ostensibly in search of material for her books, but she must have seen quite a bit. The dark groves at Vauxhall had hosted more than their fair share of illicit seduction and hasty coupling.

His mouth curved at the thought. That must be what she anticipated: a frantic bout of thrusting up against a tree, the laughter of other guests audible over the pants and moans of the copulating couple. That was rather how Bathsheba had described the encounter in Hyde Park between her heroine, Lady X, and the notorious rake pursuing her.

So did she picture herself as Lady X, willing and ready

for a quick tupping in dangerously public places? Liam thought not. The woman he knew guarded her privacy, and knew how to hold her tongue. She might think she was Lady X, might even *want* to be Lady X, but he knew better.

All his life Liam had delighted in upsetting people's view of him. His father had wanted him to be a banker, like his brother, and Liam went into newspapers. His mother wanted him to marry one of her friends' daughters, and he never managed to stay interested in a woman for more than a few months. His brother expected him to fail, or at least come beg for help, and Liam had chosen to live on bread and ale and sleep in his office when his business struggled. And now Bathsheba probably thought he would throw her on a sofa and take her like an animal, quick and to the point.

Well. Now that he pictured doing it, that might happen—eventually. His blood heated at the mental image of Bathsheba on his sofa, back arched and hair undone as he held her hips and drove into her.

But first, he meant to show her how delicate, how deliberate, and how thoroughly delicious his seduction could be.

Chapter Three

Bathsheba was sitting down, ready to work, when Liam's message arrived.

Mary, the new maid, brought it in. "Just delivered for you, ma'am," she said eagerly. "It's from Mr. MacGregor so I brought it straight up."

Bathsheba took the note she held out. It was so lovely to have servants again, after the long period of poverty, followed by the clandestine printing operation that dominated the house during production of *Fifty Ways to Sin*. Mary was a bit too interested in everything, but she was young, and she had accepted without question Bathsheba's instruction that certain messages—from Liam, mostly— must be delivered without Danny being the wiser. As much as Bathsheba might scoff about not needing her younger brother's protection, the fact remained that he was the head of their household, and if he discovered what she was doing, he would protest.

And if he could see this particular note, he might well call Liam out, Bathsheba thought as she read it.

I have been consumed by thoughts of our research endeavor, Liam wrote. It would devastate me to leave any of your hopes unsatisfied. My most ardent desire is to plumb the depths of your curiosity and show you the sublime bliss of knowledge.

She pressed her lips together. Cheeky scoundrel. She flipped the page over.

A carriage will call for you this evening at eight o'clock. —LM

Her hand shook slightly as she folded the letter and hid it in her writing desk. Tonight. Somehow she had managed not to think too much about what would happen, or how or when. But tonight . . .

She stared at her paper, blank and clean and waiting. Normally she looked forward to writing, creating exciting and dramatic obstacles for her heroine to face and overcome. She had framed Lady X's journey as a sort of Pilgrim's Progress through the dangers and temptations of England, from a fresh-faced groom out exercising his master's horse to a handsome lord whiling away a day in a quaint little hamlet while his carriage was repaired to the devilish rakes who stalked London's pleasure gardens. Lady X wasn't virtuous enough to resist them, but the object of her quest wasn't salvation—it was true and honest love. If she encountered divine pleasure along the way, so be it.

And tonight Bathsheba's goal would be just the opposite: pleasure, with a chance at true love being only a faint, wholly unexpected possibility.

She closed the lid of the desk and went to the window. Of course she didn't expect Liam to fall in love with her, and she was too old for airy dreams of true love anyway. No doubt he would be efficient and ruthless about it, as he was in everything else. She could just picture him rising from bed and asking if she had any questions.

"It's only business," she whispered to herself, staring into the brilliant morning sunshine. Only business, for him and for her. She would be poised and collected, ready to observe and learn and attentive only to the physical pleasures. That was all he'd agreed to provide, and that was all she could expect.

h

Accordingly, when the clock struck eight that evening, she was waiting in the sitting room. She wore her best gown of brown velvet, and carried a notebook and pencil in her reticule so she could make notes of any and all significant details. Liam might only allot her one or two chances to learn what she needed to know, so she mustn't squander any of it.

"Where are you going?" her brother asked when he came in.

"The assembly rooms," she lied.

Danny's face blanked. "Again? That's twice this week."

Bathsheba lifted one shoulder. "I've been in the house all day and wanted to get out."

"Oh." Looking nonplussed, he went to the side table, where the brandy was. Danny had lost his left arm at the elbow, and even though he managed quite well now, Bathsheba still watched him intently as he opened the bottle and poured a glass of liquor.

"Are you well?" she asked on impulse. Normally he didn't bat an eye when she went out.

"Of course," he shot back defensively, raising his glass.

Bathsheba waved one hand. She never offered to help him physically. When he'd come home from war, rail thin and angry at everyone for his lost limb, she had told him he was only disabled if he let himself be. "Not that. You look unhappily surprised."

He dropped into a chair. "I didn't know you were going out tonight."

"You never minded before," she pointed out.

Danny shrugged and stared into his drink. "I knew why

you were going out before. I suppose . . . Well, I suppose I didn't realize how much you liked it." He glanced up at her. "But you do, don't you?"

She hesitated. Clearly she could not tell him why she was so eager to go tonight. "What else am I to do?" He would know what she meant: no children to teach reading and arithmetic to, no husband to keep her company. Her few friends had both of those, which meant they were occupied most of the time. Most nights now, Bathsheba retired to her room to write or read by the fire with her brother, if he was at home.

Daniel's gaze shifted away at her reply. "I'm sorry, Bathsheba. It's not fair to expect you to enjoy being marooned at home with a one-armed brother."

"It's only painful when he grows maudlin," she said tartly. "Most of the time, I don't feel the suffering too acutely. We've got to look after each other, I suppose, since we've no one else."

"This life is too limited, isn't it?" He faced her again, wary but almost eager. "There's not much society."

"No." She glanced at him sideways. She'd known Danny since he was born, and she could tell from the set of his jaw that he had something on his mind. "It sounds as though you wish to change that." What did he intend, she wondered with a trace of foreboding. He'd been so revived in spirits since the production of *Fifty Ways to Sin.* Did he want to restart the newspaper business? Liam could surely tell him that was a fool's choice; Bathsheba strongly suspected her *Tales of Lady X* were subsidizing the *Intelligencer.*

"Well . . ." He paused. "Perhaps. But not without your approval, of course."

She frowned. What on earth was he talking about? It

wasn't like Danny to be so coy. But at that moment, a knock sounded on the door, sending Bathsheba's heart into her throat and scattering her thoughts. She jolted to her feet. "That'll be my hackney," she said. "Good night, Danny, don't wait up!" She pressed a quick kiss on his cheek and hurried out, leaving him staring after her in amazement.

A coachman stood on the step. Bathsheba threw on her cloak and let out her breath, relieved that Liam hadn't come himself. Not that she had expected him, but it would be like him to confound her expectations, and she would have had a thorny time explaining it to her brother, who had followed her as far as the sitting room doorway.

"Which assembly rooms?" Danny asked, suddenly suspicious.

"The usual ones," she said as she closed the door on him. "Good night!"

"Miss Crawford?" asked the coachman.

"Yes." She tugged up the hood of her cloak, even though it was warm out. "Where are we going?"

"I'm not to say." He opened the door of the waiting carriage for her, and jumped onto the box when she was settled. Bathsheba watched out the window and tried to keep track of where they went, but the carriage left London, driving past the familiar squares and thoroughfares into more rural roads before turning into a winding lane lined with oaks and finally stopping in front of a smart cottage of gray stone.

Liam was standing in the cottage doorway when the driver lowered the step and helped her down. Trying to conceal her sudden uncertainty, Bathsheba thanked the driver and crossed the neat patch of gravel. "Is this your home?"

He grinned. "Does it matter? It's private." He held out his hand. "Come in."

She avoided looking at him as she took his arm, instead examining the house with far more interest than was necessary. It was a very pleasant house, with oak floors worn shiny with time and walls of buttery yellow. Fresh flowers stood in a tall vase at the back of the small hall. "It's lovely," she said as she removed her cloak.

Liam looked around as if just noticing it. "It is, isn't it?" He hung up her cloak and put his hands on his hips. "What are you wearing, Bathsheba?"

She flushed, feeling his gaze wander down her figure. "This is my best dress."

His dark brow arched. "And you thought it was suited to a seduction?"

"If I knew what was best suited to a seduction, we wouldn't be here," she pointed out. "What ought I to have worn?"

One corner of his mouth curled, and she instinctively braced herself. Liam looked like a devil when he smiled that way, and often she thought that was his true nature, allowed to shine through for a moment. "As little as possible under the cloak. Ideally, nothing at all. But never mind that now." He turned and strode into the parlor, waving one arm for her to follow.

Grimly she went. "Nothing at all. Surely that's more appropriate when two people are already lovers, assured that the assignation will occur."

"The only reason we are not already lovers," he replied, pouring two glasses of wine, "is that this is our first assignation." He handed her a glass. "Or was that your way of saying you've reconsidered, and might not, upon further reflection, wish to proceed?"

No. The wine in her glass rippled as her hand shook. Even if she had had doubts, seeing him this way would have trampled them into dust. She had covertly admired Liam when he was at the newspaper office, his cravat pulled askew and his jacket unbuttoned as he snapped and barked at other employees. Now he wore neither jacket nor waistcoat, his neckcloth was simply knotted around his throat, and his attention was fixed on her as it never had been before.

Well—excepting that day she had made her indecent business proposal, when he agreed to make love to her.

She gulped some wine for courage. "If I didn't wish to proceed, I wouldn't have come all the way out here."

"I am gratified to hear that." His gaze raked over her once again. "Now take off that appalling dress."

She drew breath to scold him for insulting her clothing, then realized exactly what he'd said, and almost forgot to let out her breath. Very well. Right to the point; highly admirable. She set down her glass and reached for the fastenings.

"Just the gown, mind," Liam said. "And not in any great rush. We have all night." He seated himself in the middle of the sofa and began tugging his cravat loose.

Bathsheba cast a hateful glare on the lamps, burning brightly. The draperies were closed, but the door stood wide open. Defiantly she went and closed it.

Liam laughed as he flung aside his neckcloth, letting his shirt fall open at the collar. "There's no one else in the house. I do have some idea how to conduct an illicit affair."

"There was a draught," she lied. She put down her reticule and took out her notebook.

"What's that?"

"So I can record anything noteworthy."

Liam laughed again. "If you feel the need to take any notes tonight, I will have failed abysmally. Leave it."

She hesitated, but decided not to argue. She reached behind her back and pulled loose one of the tapes holding the dress closed.

"Where did you get that dress?" Liam slouched lower on the sofa, his arms spread wide of the back of it and his eyes glittering as he watched her.

"I made it. The velvet was a great indulgence." She untied the second tape.

"Why brown?"

Her fingers paused. His tone made his distaste clear. "What color should I have chosen?"

"Blue," he said softly. "Green. Even rose. You chose brown because it's unobtrusive, didn't you? Unremarkable. Not a color to seize anyone's attention and command their interest."

Bathsheba plucked at a sleeve before drawing it down her arm. "It cost less than those colors."

"Hmm." He watched as she struggled out of the gown, and that made her proceed all the slower. "Do you give no thought to how others perceive you?"

She huffed. "I know exactly how they do."

"And it pleases you, that everyone sees a plain quiet mouse of a woman?"

Bathsheba paused as he echoed the very words she had been thinking. Were her thoughts more apparent than she knew? Danny never seemed to guess, and he had known her far longer than Liam had. "I cannot control what people think, so it hardly matters to me." She finished stripping off the sleeves of her gown and untied the remaining tapes, so she could slide it down over her hips. Even though she was completely covered by her corset and petticoats, an unaccountable blush warmed her face as she stepped out of the gown and laid it aside.

"You can control what people think, far more than you believe," he said thoughtfully. "Come here."

She headed for the opposite end of the sofa, but he caught her hand and pulled her close. "Sit here," he said, gently but firmly, and spread his knees. Bathsheba flushed as she realized he meant for her to sit between his legs.

Idiot, she told herself bracingly. *You asked him to make love to you and you're as skittish as a cat to think of sitting on his knee?* She turned around and sat on the very edge of the sofa between his legs, hoping she hadn't made a big mistake.

Chapter Four

Liam was glad she was facing away from him; she couldn't see the amusement that must surely be visible on his face as she perched on the edge of the sofa, spine rigid and hands folded primly in her lap. Not a virgin, she'd said, but also not a woman of experience. He'd never known Bathsheba to be awkward or skittish, which showed how out of her depth she was tonight.

He put his hands on her waist and tugged her closer, until her bottom was snug against his groin. Hers was a very nicely rounded bottom, and Liam's anticipation of the evening jumped an alarming amount. Aside from a catch in her breathing, she made no protest. He ran his palms up her arms. Bathsheba shivered. In her plain white undergarments, she looked younger and more innocent than ever. Thank God he knew she wasn't—or at least, didn't want to be. Liam shifted his weight and reached for the pins holding her dark hair in a simple knot.

"How would you like to be seen?" He drew out one pin and set it aside.

Bathsheba started at his touch. He saw her eyes flicker toward the pin, but she didn't move. "As a decent, respectable woman."

"Decent." He drew out another pin. "What does that

mean?"

"Honorable. Honest. Kind."

"Ah." One more pin and the long braid collapsed into his hands. He plucked at the end of it, noting with mild surprise how silky soft it was. Or perhaps he hadn't paid enough attention to a woman's hair before. "And respectable?"

"The opposite of this," she said tartly, although he noticed a tremor in her shoulders as he leisurely loosened the plait.

"I am the only one who will see you like this," he replied. "The only one who will ever know, if that's what you desire."

"Of course!" She seemed to get tenser as her braid unraveled in his hands.

Liam was somewhat distracted by how sensual it was, running his fingers through her hair. There were threads of bronze in it, and he caught the faintest whiff of lavender. "Whatever you wish," he murmured.

"I wish—" She stopped and spoke in her normal voice, not a breathless rush. "I wish you would get on with it. Danny will be expecting me by a certain time, and it was a long drive here."

"Where did you tell him you were going?"

"To the public assembly rooms where I usually collect gossip."

A frown touched his brow. "You go there alone?"

An impatient sigh; she was drifting back toward her usual take-charge-and-charge-onward demeanor. "No one wants to accompany me, Liam."

"Do you wear that?" He glanced at the brown velvet dress, which really did make her look drab and insignificant.

"I told you, it's my best dress."

"Don't wear it again," he said brusquely, and then, to keep her from arguing, he leaned forward and feathered his lips down the nape of her neck.

He felt the shudder run through her; he caught the swift flexing of her forearms as her fingers clenched in her lap. He also felt a sharp zing of arousal through his own muscles. He didn't intend to make love to her tonight, but his body was ready and eager. A little too eager, to be honest—already his plan, to spend several evenings stoking Bathsheba's desire to a feverish pitch before actually taking her, seemed pointlessly restrained. She'd come here to be ravished, why shouldn't he get on with it?

Liam didn't quite know what to make of that. He was a healthy man with hearty desires. He certainly had expected that when the moment came, he would rise to it and give Bathsheba every pleasure she could imagine. But he also possessed a heretofore iron will and a strict personal discipline that seemed to have gone missing tonight.

Perhaps it was the way she had propositioned him, instead of the other way around. There was something very exciting and unexpected about a woman asking him to make love to her.

He pushed her hair forward so it spread over her shoulders, baring her back, and let his mouth roam her skin. She was warm and soft, and the touch of his tongue sent another shiver through her. Silently Liam smiled; it was damned arousing, the way she responded to the slightest thing. When he finally had her naked in his bed, she might well go up in flames.

"Not a virgin, you said," he whispered in her ear. His fingertips skated up her arms, barely contacting her flesh. "When was your first time?"

Her head was thrown back, her breathing rapid. With her hair down and her drab dress off, she looked completely unlike her usual self. Liam didn't know about decent or respectable, but she damned sure looked like a woman now.

"It was years ago." Her voice was even softer than his. "A man who worked for my father. He was charming and I was . . . curious."

"Did you enjoy it?" He ended the question by tracing a circle on the sensitive skin below her ear with his tongue. She jolted, but then slowly angled her head to the side, inviting him to repeat the action, so he did. "Did you?" he asked again.

"What? Oh—not much. It began pleasantly enough but he—he took none of the care . . ." Her voice trailed away in a quiet gasp as Liam caught her earlobe between his teeth.

"No care?"

She wet her lips. The pulse in her throat beat rapidly. "None of the care described in *Fifty Ways to Sin*. That was what caught my attention about them, you know— Constance's lovers took such care for her pleasure. William took very little for mine, although I didn't realize *how* little until later."

William. Stupid blighter. "What did he do?"

Her flush deepened, and she opened her eyes. "Does it matter?"

"I would hate to make the same mistake," Liam answered in the same low, languid voice. He ran his hands down her arms and wove his fingers through hers, lifting her hands to place them on his knees. It had the desired effect; she almost seemed to hold her breath. He slid his arms beneath hers and tugged at the string of her petticoat bodice. "Did he throw you on the sofa? Bend you over a table? Up against a wall?"

"No," she said, although her voice was tighter than it had been. "He persuaded me to take him to my bedroom, and sit on the bed with him. It was all very lovely—like this—until he—he got on top of me. A few minutes later it was over. He pulled down my skirt, kissed me on the cheek and said he'd had a wonderful time but he had to get back to work. I hardly saw him after that."

"The man should be shot," said Liam with feeling. "What a bloody arse."

She gave a short, nervous laugh. "I thought it was the most disappointing thing. I didn't expect him to stay and marry me—I never did, so I cannot blame him for that—but I thought it would be more blissful. And last a bit longer."

When he made love to her, it would last as long as she could endure. The petticoat bodice had come undone; he slid it down her arms to uncover the corset, one of the short workmanlike versions that came off in a trice. And he noted that she put her hands back on his knees without prompting once he'd got them both off her. Oh yes, this was going splendidly.

"Were there any others?"

She hesitated. "Are you going to tell me about all your previous lovers?"

Liam grinned. "If you want to hear it. But not tonight. Tonight I am learning you."

Another hesitation. "How many nights will there be?"

"I can't think how to do this properly in less than three or four nights," he said in mock indignation, taking his hands off her. "Unless you want William's version of seduction—that will only take, as you noted, a few minutes to accomplish."

"No!" She shook her head, her loose hair flying against his chest. "This way is . . . much better, so far." He grinned behind her; that last bit was so like Bathsheba, letting him know she was still reserving judgment. "There was one other. After Danny came home from the war, missing his arm, we were in very tight straits." She paused, then went on with the air of forcing out the words. "We didn't have enough to eat at times. We had lost my father's shop, my parents were dead of consumption, and then Danny lost his navy pay and his ability to work. It took him months to recover from his injury.

"Henry was a grocer. He had three children who needed a mother, and we got on well. He—he proposed to me. It would have been a very businesslike marriage," she quickly added. "I would have helped run his shop and raise his children, and he would have supported me and my brother. We were engaged for a month, and a few times we . . ." She lifted one shoulder, pronouncing silent but brutal judgment on hapless Henry's lovemaking. "I had hoped it would be better, even wonderful. That would have made me look forward to the marriage, some source of pleasure I might gain. It wasn't awful. I would call it . . . perfunctory." She paused and Liam realized he was scowling. No wonder Bathsheba adored *Fifty Ways to Sin*. Lady Constance never had so much as a perfunctory tea hour, let alone a boring or bland romp in bed.

"I think he must have been as disappointed as I was," Bathsheba went on, very quietly. "I could tell his interest in the match waned after we began sharing a bed. In truth, I broke off with him because I thought I would rather starve than become the property of a man who didn't want me."

"I can't blame you." He put his lips to her shoulder, now bare as he slowly worked her shift off. All Bathsheba's clothing was simple and easy to remove, which he appreciated. "I would have left him, too."

A bubble of laughter burst out of her. "Why?"

"If the first few times in bed are dull and unexceptional, how much worse will it get in time? Any man who doesn't put his best effort forth at the very beginning . . . Well, I fear he's a lazy, no-good sort of fellow, and I would never trust my personal satisfaction to such a man."

She turned her head to look at him, her eyes wide. Up close, he realized her eyes were as richly brown as her hair, mahogany with glints of copper. "Danny worried I'd made a terrible mistake. Henry was a respectable man, with a prosperous shop . . ."

And Liam would have bet his ownership of the *London Intelligencer* that Daniel Crawford hadn't thought for one moment of his sister's sensual appetites or feelings. "I'm sure he wanted you to be provided for, and I can't fault him for that. But I certainly wouldn't trust my brother to make the best decisions for me, so I applaud you for not blindly following his advice in that case."

Bathsheba stared at him, a startled innocence to her expression. She had not expected him to say anything like that. "Well—yes—I was proven right, in time, but *then,* you know, Danny was quite worried . . ."

"Yes," he interrupted, "but if you'd married Henry, you would never be *here,* right now." She closed her mouth, her eyes still round and unblinking. "Do you still want to be here?" he whispered. "With me? Or would you rather be with a solid, respectable husband like Henry?"

"Here," she breathed. "With you."

Liam gave her his most wicked smile. "Excellent. Stand up."

Wariness sprang into her face, but she stood up,

grasping at her clothing when it sagged toward the floor. Liam brushed away her hands and peeled the petticoat, stays, and shift down, kicking them away. Bare except for her stockings and shoes, Bathsheba's face was bright red, and she wouldn't meet his gaze. "Come," he said, pulling her back, this time facing him. She obeyed his urging and straddled him on her knees, her small breasts right in front of his face, her feminine mound tantalizingly near his groin.

For a moment the thought flashed through Liam's mind that he could undo three buttons on his trousers and be inside her right now. *It's what she wants,* whispered a little devil in his ear. *It's what you want, too . . . Take her now and teach her seduction next time . . .*

He cleared his throat to drown it out. "Put your arms around my neck."

"Why?"

He sighed, and she bit her lip. "So you won't fall off."

"Oh." Gingerly she put her hands on his shoulders, hesitated, then linked her fingers behind his neck. His hair caught in her grip for a moment, and he felt a renewed surge of lust. Would she grab his hair and hold on to him if he laid her back on the sofa and rode her right now? Would she scream and pull, urging him to be rough and primitive?

God. He was losing his mind. Four or five times? He'd be a madman by the end of tonight. He cupped her hips in both hands and pulled her right against him, her nether curls tight against his erection, separated only by his trousers. It wasn't enough, but it was better than nothing.

"Do you like your breasts?" He covered them with his hands, appreciating the firm swell and rigid peaks of her nipples.

"What?" She shook her head as if just waking up. "Why do you keep talking?"

Yes, why? Take her now, urged the devil in his brain. "I want to know. I want you to revel in everything I do to you, and in everything you're going to do to me. Next time," he added as her eyes flew wide open again.

"I thought this would be much simpler," she said in a suffocated voice.

"Then you should have asked someone else," he replied, and took one deep pink nipple between his teeth. She flinched, and he swiped his tongue over her flesh to soothe it, and began to suckle. His hands moved up and down her back, from the plump firmness of her bottom to her bowed shoulders beneath her rippling hair, urging her from side to side or back and forth as suited his explorations. She was soft and supple in his hands, moving readily. Her fingers remained knotted behind his neck, and even when he caught himself wishing she would touch him, Liam managed to keep to his plan: drive her wild. When the first sigh of rapture met his ears, he slipped his hand between their bodies and stroked the dark curls there.

Bathsheba almost leapt off his lap; Liam kept her in place with his free hand around her nape. For a second her dazed eyes met his, then she dropped her head back and began to move in time with the slow strokes of his fingers. Now that she was rocking up and down on her knees, he eased backward so he could watch. The sight of his fingers sliding into her most intimate flesh sent a bolt of heat through him; his blood was scalding him from the inside out. Jaw tight, he pushed one, then two fingers inside her, still teasing that delicate bud with his thumb. Bathsheba moaned aloud; her fingers dug into his shoulders now, her spine moving in a sinuous wave as she rode his hand.

Sweat popped out on his brow. *She wants you inside her,* screamed the devil. *Deep inside her—God, so tight—so wet.*

Desperately Liam bent his head back to her breast, laving her flesh and sucking hard, so hard there might be a mark later. And she leaned back, almost begging him, her breasts shivering and bouncing every time she breathed.

She began panting, her breath catching with every stroke. Gritting his teeth, he pushed his fingers as deep inside her as he could, withdrawing and thrusting deep again, the way he ought to be doing with a different body part. Watching feverishly, he ran his other hand over the damp curls, ruthlessly exposing the deep pink flesh and then spread that flesh open to show the pearl that held the key to her pleasure.

Speared on his left hand, driven onward by his right, Bathsheba flushed from her hair to her pretty little breasts, and rode him hard. Almost suffocating with arousal, Liam pushed her toward climax, trying to hold back his own. He'd thought this would be a bit less engrossing, a bit more scientific, but now he was nearly frantic to make her come so he could let loose the explosion building at the back of his mind.

Her arms tensed; she gasped for breath; the ripples of climax shuddered over her belly and a hot wetness covered his fingers, deep inside her. Liam cupped his right hand hard over her mound and let go, not even caring that he was spending himself in his trousers like a schoolboy. Bathsheba gave a long, sweet exclamation of release, and the world went dark around him for a moment.

Chapter Five

If Bathsheba had thought taking off her gown in front of Liam was awkward, it was nothing to the feeling when she opened her eyes after the last glorious thunderclaps of climax had died away and found herself draped over Liam, naked but for her stockings.

Good heavens.

Tentatively she tried to wiggle free, but her hands were caught behind him. He had fallen against the sofa, his head thrown back with an expression that could only be called fierce. Reality splashed over her in a cold wave. Now she was going to have to dress, probably while he watched, and then say good night. A long, chilly ride in the carriage would follow, and then she'd have to hope Danny had already gone to bed. There was no way on earth she could keep her expression neutral if her brother were waiting up to ask how her evening had gone. And if Danny found out she'd lied to him and snuck out to meet Liam, for the express purpose of debauchery, Bathsheba didn't even know how she would endure it.

Liam opened his eyes. They were a clear slate gray now. For a moment the two of them just gazed at each other, his face calm and serene and hers, no doubt, blotchy from embarrassment.

"That's lesson one," he murmured.

Stiffly she nodded.

"When do you want lesson two?"

Now. The thought streaked across her mind before she could stop it. "I can come away again on Friday," she said.

"No good," he replied, skimming one hand over her bare thigh. "I've a dinner engagement."

She frowned slightly, trying to ignore his touch. Danny would not expect her to go out on Saturday evening, and it seemed wrong to arrange an illicit rendezvous on Sunday, the Lord's Day. "Monday next?"

"Tomorrow." He grinned, lazy and tempting. "Tell Danny you've joined a sewing circle."

"He'd never believe that!" She pressed her lips together. "I don't usually go out more than once or twice a week."

"Tell him you've met someone," said Liam. "At the assembly rooms."

She raised her brows. "And when he declares he's going to accompany me the next time, to meet this hopeful suitor? Or expects the man to call on me at home? Don't be daft. Danny's got one strong arm left, and he'll draw your cork."

Liam seemed interested in that. "Would he? You think he'd disapprove of me?"

Danny would strongly—violently—disapprove of Liam taking off his sister's clothing and doing all sorts of wicked things to her. Liam's hand was still between her legs, brushing almost absently over the curling hair he had so boldly pushed aside. Something deep inside her belly contracted at the memory of his fingers moving inside her, and his mouth twitched in a satisfied smile; he knew.

Blushing, Bathsheba struggled to her feet, then felt even more exposed standing naked in front of him. She grabbed the twisted ball of undergarments and began tugging them apart. "We both know you aren't going to call in Totman Street and tell Danny I asked you to bed me."

Liam still sprawled on the sofa as if he'd just woken from a nap. Bathsheba got her shift back on and jammed her arms through the straps of her stays.

"I would hardly say that. Would he *draw my cork,* as you put it, if I simply called on you?"

"Why on earth would you do that?" She was honestly appalled. Her entire plan rested on one crucial point: no one must ever know. Liam had every reason to keep it secret. He and Danny were acquainted and knew each other well. Danny, for all that he was her younger brother, had a protective streak, and if he discovered this affair, he'd start growling at Liam to marry her. Bathsheba had promised it was only for research—and Liam had only agreed because it was to their mutual business benefit.

"It would make it easier for you to get away if you didn't have to lie to your brother," he pointed out. "I can tell him I'm escorting you to the theater."

She snorted with laughter as she yanked the strings through the stays. Liam had undone everything. "Like a courting couple? Do you want Danny to start asking about your intentions?" She shook her head and scooped up her petticoat. He didn't reply, and when she'd got the petticoat over her head and was fastening the short bodice again, she saw he wore a rather moody expression. "I don't," she hastened to assure him. "Danny's never stopped me when I go out, but he wants to know what I do or where I go, and . . . I don't like lying to him. Since I live with him, it's hard to get away without some lying. I'd rather keep the lies as small as possible."

He was quiet as she put on her velvet gown. "Whatever

you desire," he finally said, coming to his feet. He went out of the room for a minute, reappearing as she was struggling with the tapes. "The carriage will be ready soon," he said, brushing aside her hands to do them up for her. He ran his fingers through her hair, sending a tiny ripple of pleasure through her. "Do you need a comb?"

"Please."

He left the room again and Bathsheba turned around, hunting for her shoes. She caught sight of herself in the mirror above the fireplace, and stopped in shock. She looked so unlike herself; her hair was usually straight as a stick, but now it rippled over her shoulders like some kind of Botticelli goddess's. Her complexion had a healthy pink flush to it, and even her expression was different—more knowing and relaxed, perhaps, even though she still faced a long drive back home and the gauntlet that might await her there.

But surely no one could experience so much pleasure and not be affected by it. The memory of it—the tide of euphoria that had flooded her, the giddy feeling of being worshipped by Liam, the hungry cast to his face as he watched her reach the glorious peak—brought a small smile to her face. It might have begun as a business bargain, but for a moment, however fleeting, she and Liam had shared something elemental. Something deep and powerful. Something she couldn't wait to feel again, the next time they met.

Liam came back with a comb. He'd put on a banyan over his shirt and trousers, and while she re-braided her hair, he poured himself more wine and sipped it. Without a word he handed her the pins to secure her hair, in a looser knot than before, but close enough to fool Danny.

"Why do you wear your hair so tightly?" Liam asked.

She touched it self-consciously. "To keep it out of the way."

"Pity," he murmured. From the hall there came a knock on the door. "That will be the carriage."

He walked her out, helping her back into her cloak and waiting while she tied her bonnet ribbons. "Friday," he said abruptly. "Same time."

She looked at him in surprise. "Your dinner engagement . . ."

"I'll cancel it." He gave his usual sardonic smile. "Can't have you forgetting what you've learned tonight." He opened the door and picked up a lamp. As promised, the carriage that had brought her was waiting on the gravel drive.

"What did I learn tonight?" she whispered as they walked out, Liam holding the lamp for her.

He handed her into the carriage, but leaned through the open door. "How to lose yourself." He closed the door in her astonished face and rapped on the side of the carriage, which started off at once.

Bathsheba settled into the seat, feeling off balance again. Perhaps she had lost herself tonight; it hadn't been what she expected. Her little notebook was completely empty of helpful notes and ideas for her next book. But Liam was willing to cancel a dinner engagement to see her again— what did he plan for lesson two? Something fizzed inside her chest, nervous and excited at the same time. Three days had never sounded so long.

Liam threw himself into work for the next three days. The evening with Bathsheba—or lesson one, as he kept calling it in his mind—had been more affecting than expected, and he didn't want to drive himself mad from dwelling on it. He had not expected her to be so passionate, or so willing. But then he would ask himself what he *had* expected, and there was no answer. Why wouldn't she be willing, when she proposed the whole exercise? Why shouldn't she be passionate, given that she knew passion was lacking in her own life, but still craved it?

But when Friday morning dawned, he washed and dressed with more care than usual and had his valet trim his hair. At the first meeting, he had wanted to learn Bathsheba—what pleased her, what aroused her, how she reacted to him. Tonight he wanted her to learn him. It had sounded like a good plan when he came up with it, but now the thought of Bathsheba stripping him, touching him, putting her mouth on him . . . It was enough to make him lose his line of thought entirely and send two reporters out on crossed assignments.

When he closed the office, he headed for Wharton's Bank, where his accounts were. Unfortunately it was also where Angus was a partner, although Liam was careful never to do business directly with his brother. He saw Niall Wharton instead, handing over a list of the transfers and payments he needed made. Even though Niall was a partner as well—son of the founder, in fact—he and Angus didn't get on that well. It was enough to assure Liam than Niall would keep his mouth closed around Angus.

But today Angus must have been idle, because as soon as Liam stepped out of Niall's office, his brother was there. "Come to hide from all the ladies wanting to seduce you?" he asked with a smirk.

Liam paused. "Why on earth would I hide from them, rather than from you?"

Angus scowled. "Admit it, man. No such thing has ever

happened to you. I've queried every man I know, and not a one has ever had a woman throw up her skirts for him—absent a marriage proposal, that is."

"That," said Liam gravely, "is a reflection of what a sorry lot of mates you have, Angus."

"If you're going to make up rubbish, at least make up a description." Angus followed him through the bank, like a dog after a bone. "It cannot be that lovely blonde you met here from time to time."

"You know it's not." Liam smirked at the mention of Madeline Wilde. "She's married another man, and I assure you, I was never more than a business partner to her." Although one might have said the same of Bathsheba, until a few days ago.

That seemed to calm Angus. "Of course not! She's a beauty, that one, but a wee bit cold. Although, it surely couldn't have been business alone on your mind, all those times you met her here . . ."

"It was," returned Liam evenly. "Her husband owned part of my newspaper. When he died, it became hers. I meet her to disclose information about her share of the *Intelligencer.*" And also to collect the gossip column she wrote for him, under strictest secrecy. Liam didn't know if that arrangement would endure much longer, as Madeline had recently married Douglas Bennet, heir to a wealthy baronet and one of the most notorious, though eligible, men in London. Liam had never tried to woo Madeline—her first husband had been more of a brother to him than Angus, so it would have been like seducing his sister-in-law—but he was not surprised at all that a rakehell like Bennet would set his sights on her. He *was* surprised that Madeline had fallen for Bennet, but one never could tell with women when it came to love. Even Bathsheba might be susceptible to it, if the right man were to take aim at her.

Angus harrumphed. "You're a bloody liar. You never thought of it: ha! Now you claim women all over London are offering you a tumble, but you can't even say what they look like. Bloody liar," he repeated for good measure.

Liam stopped and made a show of glancing around, as if for privacy. "Hair like silk," he said, so quietly Angus had to lean closer. "Long and wavy, and when she's wearing nothing else . . ." He inhaled meaningfully. "Eyes warm and inviting. Skin as soft as a peach. And a mouth that would make your brain cease working, when you imagine it touching yours."

Angus was barely breathing. "No . . ."

Liam smiled and touched the brim of his hat. "Good day, Angus." He walked out, reveling at leaving his older brother speechless. There was no good reason for Angus to be so interested in Liam's love affairs; Angus had a fiancée, a perfectly respectable woman called Miss Lachlan whose mother was one of Mrs. MacGregor's dear friends. Unfortunately Miss Lachlan's father had died two weeks before their planned wedding this past spring, so the marriage had been postponed until after her mourning was finished. Angus must be feeling ill-natured because he ought to have had his own woman to bed by now, but didn't. The Lachlans were rather pious people and Miss Lachlan wanted to observe a full year for her father.

Which was a terrible pity for poor Angus, but not Liam's problem. He hailed a hackney and gave the direction of his little house in the village of St. John's Wood. He'd bought it for privacy, and because it was more affordable to live so far from town. It was also something of a secret; all his correspondence went to the *Intelligencer* offices or to Wharton's Bank, and he lived quietly, even reclusively, avoiding the few neighbors. Tonight that seemed like a brilliant decision.

He'd left orders that morning with his housekeeper, and arrived home to find everything ready. A cold plate of dinner was waiting under a cloth in the dining room, and the servants had taken their night out. He ate and then strolled through the house, viewing it critically. The sofa in the parlor had proved adequate, but he wanted to keep Bathsheba off guard. He thought of what he had in mind for her second lesson and realized he was staring at the long, wide chaise in his small library. It was extremely comfortable for reading, with his feet propped up and a pillow behind his back. He wouldn't be reading tonight . . . but this would suit him perfectly. Smiling, he went to fetch the wine.

Chapter Six

Friday threw Bathsheba into a crisis unlike any she had ever suffered before: one of fashion.

For three days she had successfully put her "lessons" from her mind. Despite the lack of notes, her writing had been almost frantically inspired this week. She'd written close to fifty pages of her next tale, and they were rather high quality pages if she did say so herself. Far from growing dull or routine, her heroine's encounter felt daring and charged. Never had writing been so easy or so exhilarating. She would have to consider taking a lover more often, as it appeared to have refreshed her entire creative spirit.

But on Friday she had to confront one point that had nagged at her those three days. She did not have an attractive dress. Why this mattered, she wasn't sure, but Liam's derision of her brown velvet began to assume unreasonable importance in her mind. It didn't matter if he found her attractive or well-dressed, she tried to tell herself. She'd only take off the dress soon after she arrived, and it could offend no one lying on a chair. But she still found herself scowling into her wardrobe, irrationally distressed that all her clothes were practical and plain.

"Are you going out again?" asked Mary, hovering in the

doorway.

"Yes, but I don't know what to wear." She touched a rust-colored dress, then a dark blue. They were both new, bought to replace dresses ruined by ink while they were printing *Fifty Ways to Sin* in the cellar, but suddenly Bathsheba thought them both old and tired. Or perhaps she was the problem, too plain and dull to look attractive in anything. She sighed. This should not matter to her. Liam knew perfectly well that she was plain and unfashionable when he agreed to this.

"Where are you going?"

"Oh—a dinner party," she said, blushing at the lie. "But don't tell Mr. Crawford," she added quickly. "It's a philosophical society and my brother doesn't hold with such things." Fortunately Danny was accustomed to spending Friday evenings at the local pub, so she wouldn't have to lie to him directly.

"Then you want to look lovely." Mary opened the wardrobe doors wider and pulled out a dress. "This one is handsome."

Bathsheba laughed in surprise. "It's several years old!" It had once been her favorite, but now was hopelessly out of fashion.

Mary shook out the sage green skirt, spreading it out for examination. "It's still in fine condition, and it suits you, ma'am." She held it up. "It looks like it will fit."

Dubiously, Bathsheba considered it. "You think so?" It was a simple round gown, at least ten years old. She remembered wearing it before her parents' deaths, when she'd been young and hopeful. Surely such a gown would look ridiculous on a woman of her age. Aside from some white embroidery around the sleeves and bodice, it was unadorned.

"We'll add a ribbon for a sash. With a necklace, you'll be quite lovely, ma'am." Mary's round face shone eagerly, and Bathsheba found herself agreeing to try it.

Even after discovering it still fit—one benefit to being poor was that she hadn't put on much weight—and even after Mary produced a long black ribbon sash that lent a sophisticated air to the ensemble, Bathsheba fidgeted. Mary rolled her hair into a simple chignon and pinned it at the nape of her neck, softer than her usual scraped-back style. Even to Bathsheba's critical eyes, she looked better than usual, but part of her recoiled from it. This wasn't a romantic assignation with Liam, it was a business meeting.

During which she expected to end up naked and shuddering in sensual release.

This time the ride in the carriage seemed shorter than before. When she stepped down, her hands were just as shaky as the first time, and the fact that Liam stood in the doorway waiting, just as before, made her somehow feel gauche and shy.

Things improved when she took off her cloak. The expression on his face said she'd been right to trust Mary. "Much better," he said with approval.

"It's old," she said for no reason.

"But still more appealing than the brown. Come." He led the way to another room, a library where a fire burned against the chill of the evening and two glasses of wine stood on the table. This time he closed the door. "No draughts," he said with a slight smile, and Bathsheba flushed scarlet.

"Any regrets?" He handed her a glass of the wine, and she took a nervous sip. "I am open to any critique, now that you've had a few days to reflect upon lesson one."

"No. No regrets." She twisted the glass in her hands.

"You?"

He laughed. "None at all."

That buoyed her courage a little. "Then shall we begin?"

"Drink some wine," he said with amusement. "I think you'll be glad later."

What did that mean? Her fevered imagination bolted like a startled horse, rampaging through various erotic visions. Her knees started to quake, and her heart banged inside her chest, and she gulped down some wine.

"Is this your house?" she asked, trying to distract herself from anticipation of what lay ahead.

Liam hesitated. "It is."

"It's quite handsome," she said truthfully. "And so pleasantly removed from London."

"That was crucial." A wry smile crossed his face as he glanced around the room. "It's not widely known, so it's quite private."

Bathsheba nodded, drinking again. She understood what he was saying, both assuring her of discretion and urging her to keep it. "Good." Her glass was almost empty. "Should I take off my dress now?"

His gaze slithered over her. "Take it off or leave it on, as you wish."

"Oh?" She almost choked on the last mouthful of wine. "We won't—? That is, aren't you—?"

He took the glass out of her limp fingers. "Tonight you're going to undress me. If you also wish to disrobe . . ." He flashed his lazy smile. "I will not object."

Oh dear Lord. The thought of Liam, naked, sent her pulse leaping so hard, she thought she might faint. "That is not what I asked for," she blurted out.

"Seduction goes both ways," he countered. "At least, it should." He folded back one shirt cuff and undid it, then undid the other one. He dropped the studs on the mantel. "Or do you find it unappealing?"

No. She found the idea dangerously, lusciously appealing, and she feared the actual experience of it would leave her a lunatic, mad with lust for him. "Don't be silly," she said brusquely. "You're the bloody expert, I'll follow your recommendation."

He was still smiling, the rotter. Bathsheba vowed to take that smile off his face. "Very well. Undress me—but leisurely. As you imagine a woman would undress her lover."

If I could make myself your lover, I would, she thought. "And I keep all my clothes on?"

"As many as you wish," he agreed.

She reflected a moment. "Are there any benefits to disrobing?"

His eyes gleamed. "By all means, bare anything you wish to offer up for my enjoyment."

The thought of lesson one being repeated while he was as naked as she was blazed across her mind. His hands on her bare flesh felt incredible; she was dying to feel his skin. "Very well," she said, and untied her sash. She removed her dress and petticoat, but paused after laying them aside. "That's enough for now," she announced, then cringed.

He only smiled at her nerves. "Now my clothes," he prompted. He wore a banyan over trousers and shirt, no jacket or waistcoat or even boots; he wore slippers on his bare feet. Bathsheba pushed the banyan down his shoulders, then tugged at his cravat.

"Gently," he murmured. "And try not to look so grim as you do it."

Her hands paused. "I've never done this before," she said tartly. "Perhaps you should describe the process before

I attempt it."

"Imagine yourself Lady Constance," he said after a moment. "Finally alone with the man you desire. You're anxious to strip him to your gaze, eager to marvel at his body—but patient enough to savor each moment of the unwrapping. You want your lover to take his time with your pleasure; take your time with his. Explore at will."

Explore. He was giving her carte blanche with his body. A rapid pulse of excitement throbbed through her, in her belly and lower. She untied his cravat with steady hands, although she avoided his gaze. It was strange enough to be undressing him without gazing into his eyes the whole while. That felt too lover-like, too intimate. They were not lovers, this was not true intimacy, and she didn't want to take one step down the path toward letting herself think it was.

The shirt buttons came loose with a flick of her fingers; she gathered the fabric at his waist and pushed upward until his bare abdomen was beneath her hands.

And oh—she almost forgot herself. Bathsheba pushed the shirt up and up, over his head until he pulled out his arms and she let it drop to the floor. He was solid and well-muscled, with a light mat of dark hair covering his upper chest and narrowing down his stomach. Bathsheba had seen naked statues in museums, and she had cared for her brother in his illness. Liam left them all in the shade and took her breath away.

"Explore," he reminded her, and without thinking she plowed her fingers through the hair on his chest. It was soft but crisp, not thick but evenly spread, and she stepped closer, fascinated by the texture.

"May I put my mouth on you?"

His stomach flinched. "Yes." Bathsheba leaned forward

and touched her tongue to his small, flat nipple. Liam's abdomen flexed again, but he didn't protest. She gave a gentle pull with her teeth, then sucked it between her lips as he had done to her. The flesh grew ripe and hard against her tongue, and when she drew back, she noticed his other nipple was hard as well, standing out from the sprinkling of dark hair. She stroked her thumb over it, then pinched it lightly.

"Do you like that?" She glanced up at him.

His gray eyes were hooded. "Can't you tell?"

She blushed. "I didn't know . . ."

"That it would be the same for a man as for a woman?" His knowing little smile was back. "It is."

Annoyed, she pressed her lips to his skin, pulling the hard little nub tight against her teeth. His breath hissed, and when she peeked at his face, his eyes had grown dark and focused on her. Her hands wandered freely, exploring the firmness of his muscles, marveling at how warm he was, how large, how male. Boldly she undid the buttons on his trousers, and pushed the fabric down. Without a word he kicked off his slippers and stepped out of the garment, and let her strip down his drawers.

For the rest of her days, Bathsheba would remember the moment. Tall, dark, unspeakably handsome, he stood before her completely unabashed by his nudity or rampant arousal. His arms flexed slightly as she stared, gorging her eyes on the sight. His hair fell around his face, lending him a rather savage air as he gazed at her.

"May I?" Her question came out husky with desire. She gestured toward his erection, jutting thick and long from his groin.

"As you wish," he said in a deep growl, and she felt a surge of elation at the hunger in his voice.

She ran her fingers down his stomach, feeling a small thrill at the way it contracted, and into the thatch of dark hair. His body was so much harder than hers, everywhere. She explored the lean lines of his hips, and wrapped her hands around his bottom, remembering how he had handled her body so boldly and possessively. But she didn't touch his erection; she was trying to tease him as he had teased her. Every covert glance she stole at his face, though, revealed nothing about her success. His expression was dark and fixed as he watched her with scorching intensity. Finally she gave in and stroked her palm down the length of his member.

His chest expanded. At last—a reaction. She did it again, then circled him with both hands at once. So smooth, so vital. She could almost see the blood throbbing beneath the delicate skin. She had touched a man before, but never so brazenly, never so deliberately.

Perhaps this was what he had felt last time, when he seemed to be bent on torturing her by touching her slowly and lightly when she wanted more. Feeling a little drunk, she went down on her knees and touched her tongue to him.

"Bloody—" He cut off the curse and flung out one hand to grip the mantel. His head fell back and he seemed to be struggling to breathe. A delighted smile crossed her face. She had read about this act, though had certainly never tried it, and the one invariable part of the stories was how much a man enjoyed it. According to *Fifty Ways to Sin*, it made a man absolutely delirious with pleasure. She took him between her lips and sucked as he had sucked on her skin.

"Bathsheba," he gasped. "What—?"

She paused. "You said I could touch you as I wished,

and put my mouth on you."

The muscles in his arms bulged. His knuckles grew white where he held the mantel. "Yes," he said after a moment, his voice tight. "Yes, I—I did say that. I simply didn't expect . . ." His words choked off as she repeated her earlier action.

Unfortunately the description she'd read had been a little lacking in specifics. Driven by the greedy rapture in Liam's face, she played at it for a few minutes, but soon ran out of ideas. Suck more? Her jaw was beginning to cramp. Lick more? He reacted less to that. And the deepest darkest secret in her breast was that she wanted to induce a reaction from him. A reaction that would leave him dazed with wonder and filled with growing joy that she was not merely Bathsheba, the woman who wrote the naughty stories that made money for him, but Bathsheba, a woman whose passionate hopes and dreams matched his own. It would take so little for her to fall helplessly in love with him, and for a moment the longing for any sign at all that he might look fondly on her was overpowering.

Sense resurfaced quickly, thank heaven. He was not going to fall in love with her, and therefore she must do everything in her power to guard against falling in love with him. She rose from her knees and resumed touching him everywhere but there, where he was still glistening wet from her mouth.

Some of the tension drained from his body as well. His breathing grew deep and even again, although he didn't release the mantel until she asked, "What now?"

A feral smile. "Explored to your satisfaction?"

I could never get enough of you. "For now," she said.

"Good." He led her to the chaise, and told her to sit. Bathsheba perched on the edge, but he knelt, picked up her foot, and spread her legs until she was straddling the chaise. "Lie back," he said, holding her knees in place.

She eased backward onto the pile of pillows, feeling more exposed than ever even though she still wore her stays and chemise, which she tried to push discreetly down to cover herself. But Liam brushed her hands aside and folded the chemise back until she was naked to the waist.

And then he sat back and stared at her nether regions. Even though he'd touched her there last time, Bathsheba blushed fiery red.

"Don't be embarrassed," he murmured. "You're very pretty here." His knuckles brushed the springy curls.

"Like all your other lovers?" She stared at the ceiling, trying not to feel like an idiot.

"You keep mentioning them. Stop."

"This is all new to me," she flared out, "but not to you!"

He paused. "It is new," he said. "*You* are new."

She realized what he was going to do a moment before he lowered his head. Her stomach seized, almost cramping with excitement and anxiety as he kissed the inside of her thigh. Lady Constance wrote of this—oral pleasure—in rhapsodic terms. Bathsheba squeezed her eyes shut, hardly breathing as he licked his way up her thigh, nibbling once or twice. He laid his palm on her mound, making her jump, and then he pushed back the curls and laid his lips right against the center of pulsing want.

Bathsheba's back arched; her mouth fell open. Liam's hand on her pelvis pushed her back down, wide open to his questing tongue. Softer, wetter, hotter than his fingers, he explored as if he meant to take all night. Shaking from the raw intimacy of it, desperate for him to do more, she writhed and rocked on the chaise.

He raised his head and waited until she managed to

open her eyes and look at him. "You like this," he whispered. She gave a tiny nod. "So do I." He grinned. "You taste sweet." He hooked both hands over her thighs, pushing them even wider apart, and lowered his mouth— teasing no longer, but insistent and demanding.

Later Bathsheba thought she might have clawed rents in the upholstery of the chaise. Liam suckled on her, refusing to let her retreat from his most wicked kiss. When she thought she would faint from the intensity of it, he would relent, his tongue turning soft and gentle, but only for a moment. It seemed as if her every muscle was drawn up tight and hard, and then he plunged his fingers inside her, as thick and hard as last time. Bathsheba screamed as the pleasure crested, swamping her.

As if from a distance she heard him swear under his breath, then he rose up over her, shoving her shift aside. He planted his hands beside her shoulders and let his weight fall on her. His eyes glowed in the firelight as he thrust his hips, grinding his rigid erection against her belly. Some primal instinct made her push her hips upward into his, and his head fell back. Two, three, five thrusts later he shuddered, and spilled himself on her skin.

Chapter Seven

For a long minute neither moved. Liam's arms were slick with perspiration, braced beside her. Her own arms were clasped around his waist, holding him to her, and one of her legs had got hooked around his. Bathsheba felt wrung out and limp, unable to move, but also uninterested in changing her situation. She'd suspected last time that he had found his own release, but this time there was no doubt. Something deep inside her purred in satisfaction; he was as aroused by this as she was.

Of course, that might not be due to her particular person; any female body might do the same. Bathsheba could not stop herself from hoping it was the former, even slightly, as she told herself it was more likely the latter. Liam was a handsome man, worldly and wicked. He hadn't had one thought of doing this with her until she badgered him into it.

"So," she said breathlessly, to drive those thoughts away, "that was lesson two, I take it."

He raised his head. "Yes." And he grinned, so joyfully she had the mad thought that he might kiss her. His lips were only a few inches from hers, and her chin even tipped upward, unconsciously rising to meet him because the only way this evening could improve was if he did kiss her—

everything else was mere physical release, but a kiss would mean honest affection—

"I'll ring for the carriage." He ran one fingertip down her cheek, then pushed himself up and off her. He fetched a handkerchief and gently wiped her belly clean. Shrugging into his banyan, he walked out of the room.

Stupid girl, she chided herself, sitting up and touching her hair, now a wild mess. When would she stop hoping? *Perhaps never,* her foolish heart whimpered. With a sigh she got up and collected her clothes.

By the time he returned she was dressed and had let down her hair, for Mary's chignon was ruined beyond repair. Without a word he handed her the comb, and she twisted up her hair into its usual simple knot. When she turned from the mirror, he had poured more wine and was watching her from across the room. It did terrible things to her composure when he did that. She wasn't used to people watching her, for one thing, but especially not Liam watching her with his all-knowing eyes, perhaps picturing how she looked on her knees before him. Or how she looked writhing like a wanton while he drove her mad with his mouth. Or how she looked right now, plain and drab and desperate, like a woman who couldn't attract a lover in the usual way, but had to argue a man into it.

She fiddled with the comb, then set it aside. "Will lesson three include consummation?" she asked. "Or more of this pretend seduction?"

His eyebrows went up. "Pretend seduction?"

"Yes," she replied. "You don't have to seduce me. You know I'll let you have me—I asked you to do it. All this . . ." She hesitated. "This *exploration* is lovely, but quite unnecessary. I merely wanted to experience the euphoric side of lovemaking—"

"And you haven't found pleasure so far," he cut her off. "Is that it?"

She blushed. "No, of course I have. I just didn't expect it to take this long—"

"The quicker the act, the shorter the pleasure."

Her face was on fire as he shredded her arguments in that dry, cynical tone. "I wouldn't know," she snapped, "since we've not done *the act*. Would you just get on with it?" She was beginning to think she had made a terrible mistake. Yes, these "lessons" had been pleasurable beyond her dreams. The longer they went on, though, the harder it was to keep her head clear and her heart safe. The best thing she could do was speed the lessons along as quickly as possible, so she could hold her head high and maintain her dignity in the months and years to come, when she would still be working with Liam.

But he looked wildly annoyed. His eyes narrowed and his mouth formed a flat line. "Very well. As you wish."

As you wish. He'd been saying that all evening, and since the one thing she *did* wish more than anything—the one thing she most did not *want* to wish—had not happened and probably never would, her patience snapped. "Yes, I do wish," she retorted. "Briskly and efficiently."

His gaze turned cool. "As you wish," he said again, making her want to scream. "Come back a week from tonight. Plan to stay the entire night."

She gaped. "What? No! I cannot!"

"Then you ought to find someone else." From the hall came a loud rap at the front door. "The carriage is ready." Without looking at her, Liam walked into the hall, leaving her to storm after him in frustration.

"I only meant you don't need to spend so much time on it," she said, trying to placate him. "I know you're a busy man! Three nights is already more than I expected you to grant me, and I'm grateful enough that I don't want to try your patience."

"And yet you are." He handed over her cloak and bonnet. The sash of his banyan had slipped, and she could see he still wore nothing underneath. The wild temptation to put her hands under the silk and *explore at will* nearly made her faint. Perhaps if he found as much pleasure in this as she did, he would want to prolong it—perhaps that accounted for his maddeningly slow pace.

And perhaps he had to work his way up to it, teaching her something about being a good lover so she wouldn't be inept and disappointing beneath him when the time came.

"Then I am sorry," she said, huddling into her cloak and tying the bonnet ribbons with unsteady hands. "It was not my intent."

Liam paused. "No? Then what was your intent? Did you hope I would throw you on the nearest horizontal surface and take you fast and hard? That's not what you asked. You asked for deeper knowledge. By your own account you're acquainted with the mechanics of the deed; I understood it was the pleasure of the deed you were missing. My intent was to show you that. If I have been mistaken and you only wanted a few more tumbles to check your memory's accuracy, then by all means find a willing fellow at the assembly rooms. I daresay most of the blokes there will accept with alacrity and then not remember your face the next day, preserving the secrecy you requested." He opened the door, revealing the carriage waiting. "If you want what I can teach you, come back a week from tonight—and plan to spend the entire night."

Mortified and furious, she blinked back tears and dropped a curtsey in mock deference. "Yes, sir. I will notify you of my decision in a few days."

"Notify me only if you won't come," he said as she swept out of the house. "Otherwise I'll see you in a week." And he closed the door without waiting to see her off.

Bathsheba flung herself into the coach, alternating between numb shock and steaming fury. *Find someone else! Stay the whole night!* What kind of woman did he think she was? What sort of man was he?

The man I want, her stupid heart mourned. Cold, calculating, sensual, wicked, and unquestionably the focus of her innermost desires. Bathsheba slumped against the carriage seat, exhausted, and wondered how she would contrive to get away for an entire night.

Chapter Eight

Liam brooded over her words. Briskly and efficiently! What sort of woman wanted that? Not that he hadn't thought of taking her roughly and quickly, especially after she closed her soft pink lips around his erection and suckled so hard her cheeks hollowed out. He'd been about three seconds away from throwing her onto the hearth rug and riding her to the hardest, fastest climax of her life, and had counted himself very virtuous for restraining that urge.

And that, perhaps, was the problem. He was not accustomed to virtue; it didn't suit him. He wanted Bathsheba. Even worse, he wanted her more desperately every time he saw her.

That was not what he had expected. At first he had thought there was a chance she would change her mind and decide she didn't want to continue, after lesson one. She'd come apart in his hands, and deep inside Liam knew it would forever alter their relationship. He didn't think he would be able to read her manuscripts without imagining that Bathsheba was Lady X and he was her lover, whoever that lover was, whether they were embracing against a tree in Hyde Park or on the finest linen sheets in Lady X's town house. It wouldn't stop him from publishing her tales—that would be stupid, as those stories accounted for a significant percentage of his income—but it would be an image lodged in his mind forever.

Then tonight, he'd thought she was embracing the spirit of the enterprise, unflinching in her admiration of his body. Liam had felt that to the marrow of his bones, the realization shocking him but also enthralling him. This was a side of Bathsheba he'd not guessed at. It was one thing for her to respond to his touch and follow where he led her. Tonight she was the leader, and he thought she *could* make him lose all sense if she kept it up. Perhaps this relationship didn't need to expire after she'd satisfied her curiosity. They were both discreet adults, living in the same town and well able to contrive reasons to see each other. This could become a lasting affair, stretched over as many sensual months as pleased them both.

But then she'd gone mad: *would you just get on with it?* She didn't want the affair to last. She wanted a quick coupling, maybe two, so she could get back to her life and not be hampered by coming out to St. John's Wood and spending the night in ecstasy with him.

He stalked back into the library, where things had gone so splendidly until her last outburst, and scowled at the scene. His clothing was scattered on the floor where she had thrown it—she might be innocent but she wasn't shy. He dropped the banyan and snatched up his shirt to fling it over his head, then stepped into his trousers. Was the woman totally deranged? She asked him to show her passion and pleasure, then grew impatient when he did so. Liam knew she'd had the best climax of her life. When she screamed in release and he threw himself on top of her to ease his own raging lust, he'd seen the awestruck wonder on her face. Whoever her inept previous lovers had been, Liam was very certain neither of them had ever made her scream like that.

His gaze fell on the chaise. He could still picture her sprawled on the pillows, legs spread wide, all that silky wavy hair lying around her, her eyes starry and her mouth pink. He could still taste her on his lips, and he could still feel the hot suction of her mouth on his erection. God. What more could any woman want than the incendiary passion they shared?

There was something under the chaise. He reached down and picked up her reticule, a sturdy plain bag of dark gray wool. He pulled the string and looked inside, not surprised when he shook out a small notebook and short pencil. She'd planned to take notes again, even after the first lesson.

Liam knew he had a reputation for being cold. He preferred to think of himself as focused, rational, and logical in every situation. In fact, he thought Bathsheba was like him in that; her practical streak went bone deep, and once her mind fastened on a problem or question, she would pursue it until she conquered it. He flipped through the little book, wondering what she would have written, and saw, with some surprise, it was half full of notes already.

He shouldn't read it.

He shouldn't even *look* at it.

He sat down on the end of the chaise and opened to the first page.

It began with scribbled ideas for her next book. He'd read the first few chapters of that manuscript and recognized the plot and character names. Then came a list of queries, some answered, some not, about practical matters: *schedule of mail coaches to Kent? Ease of sailing from Deal to Calais? Visit British Museum and assess possibilities for rendezvous locations.* The last made him smile, picturing Bathsheba striding through the museum, her head swiveling from side to side in search of an alcove or closet where two people could conceivably be intimate, briskly and efficiently.

He kept reading. Her notes changed as she wrote more of the book, deciding that Lady X would not meet a lascivious country vicar after all, but a strapping blacksmith instead, when her horse threw a shoe. *A rough man, powerful and large in all ways,* she'd written, a faint line under the word *all.* Liam smirked; he knew what that meant, but had Bathsheba? She must have done, but now he was very curious to read those chapters of the tale. Without thinking, he picked up the pencil.

Make him a clever fellow—a gentleman's bastard, educated with his half-brother or similar—or else it will seem coarse and depraved of Lady X, he wrote. *Surely you don't expect her to be satisfied by an ordinary brute.*

He turned ahead and read more. Several queries about fashion, which he mostly skipped, and a few about the timing of certain events. Bathsheba delighted in working in mentions of notable occasions, and in two places she had copied in reports of a ball and an art viewing for possible inclusion.

Liam made a few more notes—*consider some public spectacle, such as the King's progress to Parliament, as a way to introduce her to a new gentleman*—and was feeling entertained by the whole thing when he reached the last pages with writing.

Seduction, read the title on one page. *Clothing or not? Who removes? What clothing is most suitable?* There was space below, but no answers.

Timing, read the next page. *Duration of the act? What*

shortens or lengthens? How long does seduction last before, and what does one do after?

Again there were no answers.

Damn.

Slowly Liam turned another page. Location was the next subject. Is a bed the best place? What other options? Can it be done against a wall? In the manner of animals? Benefits and drawbacks of various positions?

But the worst, Liam discovered, was the last. Kissing was the title, and it was underlined heavily. Is it important? How does one do it well? What does it mean for the rest? Why do men avoid it? Is it a sign of true affection?

Liam ran one hand over his face. *Bollocks.* He couldn't pretend he'd never read it, because he'd rashly written on earlier pages. But he sensed Bathsheba would be both furious and humiliated if she knew he'd seen these notes on seduction, these questions she'd yearned so desperately to answer that she asked him to make love to her.

Was it only for her writing? Liam had never really thought so, but he had to admit he hadn't spent much time wondering exactly how much of her motivation was due to the tales and how much sprang from her own personal desires. Now . . . he wondered. She'd only known lovemaking from a callous seducer and a grocer more in search of a mother for his children than a woman to love and cherish. Bathsheba had told him from the start that she wasn't a virgin, but Liam thought she'd only forsaken that condition on technical grounds; she'd never known passion or even physical satisfaction in her liaisons. And now he suspected no one had ever really kissed her.

Including him.

He surged to his feet, recoiling from that. That was not a fair comparison. He deliberately hadn't kissed her. She said she only wanted some experience of lovemaking itself, as if a few encounters would answer all her questions about how it ought to be done. She'd never mentioned kissing, or embraces, or anything else that might hint at a deeper connection.

He hadn't kissed her because she didn't want to fall in love with him, and therefore he didn't want to fall in love with her.

And yet . . . he'd wanted to kiss her. When he put her in the carriage a few nights ago, the thought had crossed his mind. Tonight, after he'd spent himself against her belly, imagining all the while he was driving himself inside her, he'd come within a moment of kissing her when she looked up at him with glowing brown eyes and said something about lesson two. It was so like her, and so like him, that he'd wanted to laugh and kiss her and repeat the lesson all over again. He'd had the unexpected thought that he'd finally met a woman who thought the way he did, who understood—and wanted—him as he was . . .

Perhaps she did—too much so. It was the memory of her businesslike demeanor at the start that kept him from crossing the line. But as much as Liam told himself this had begun as pure business for him—well, pure business with a healthy dose of curiosity, and perhaps a little delight at being pursued . . . Damn it, it had never been pure business. He'd spent more time this past fortnight thinking about seducing Bathsheba than he'd ever spent on another woman.

He looked at the little book. Did she want kissing? Did she want him to kiss her, or had that page been written before she decided to ask him to show her passion? And— come to think of it—who else had she considered? Had she asked other men and been turned down? Liam realized he was scowling at that thought; what bloody bastards would turn her down? Bathsheba was the cleverest woman he knew, as well as the most sensible; she knew when to hold her tongue and when to carry a conversation. She was quick to recognize a business opportunity, immensely practical and capable, but also liable to turn into a bold and uninhibited lover with the slightest encouragement.

The only reason he could think of was that she was not a beauty. Well—not until a man saw her naked, hair wild about her shoulders, with her face flushed and her eyes gone liquid after a shattering climax. Something primal growled in his chest that he had been able to bring her to that point, that no other man had been a skilled enough lover to do it, but he had seen her that way. She'd been beautiful then, on his lap with her arms around his neck. Under him on the chaise, with her fingernails digging into his arse.

He slid the little book into his pocket, suddenly afraid she would not come back next week at all.

The week passed in a blur. Bathsheba found herself hideously distracted, unable to concentrate on her work. At times she would feel furiously angry with Liam, and resolve that she would not go back at the end of the week, nor would she ever again mention the subject to him. She'd done well enough making things up so far, and she could keep on doing so, thank you very much. Perhaps Liam would think she'd taken his advice and found some other man to do what he hadn't. Yes, let him think that; she even wrote a draft of a letter implying that very thing, just to put him in his place and demonstrate that she was not going to tolerate his high-handed attitude at all.

Then she threw the note in the fire, because she knew Liam and if she hinted that she'd been letting other men make love to her, he'd ask where and who and when. At best he would be annoyed that she'd wasted his time instead of finding some other fellow from the start, and at worst he'd tease her and ask horrible questions she wouldn't be able to answer. And of course it was impossible to think of asking another man to do what Liam had done.

She never should have started down this road. Much better if she'd asked a stranger to do it, for then she wouldn't have to see her former lover every week and know what he looked like in the throes of passion or how his skin tasted, or how his hands felt moving over her skin, driving her wild, thrusting deep inside her. She wouldn't be dying of anguish because she still wanted him months from now, after these lessons were over, or because her silly heart would probably always hold out some tiny hope that someday, somehow, he might fall in love with her. If she'd asked another man, some careless rake who wouldn't remember her name the next day, her secret infatuation with Liam could have continued undisturbed and forever unfulfilled.

She wrote another note, this time on dry impersonal business matters. This was to show that she was capable of carrying on with life even with this unfinished affair between them, and that she had not turned into a silly female mooning over him now that he'd given her a few climaxes. She read the note again, realized the entire thing could be read as an oblique metaphor for coupling, and that letter joined the first on the fire.

After four days she realized her choices were few: let go of the whole mad idea and try to regain the comfortable business relationship they'd had before, or figure out how she would be able to spend an entire night away from home without Danny rousing the constabulary.

She hadn't been exaggerating when she told Liam it would be difficult. When she and Danny had set up house together originally, he had been still recovering from losing his arm. He was a year younger than she, and she had been terrified that he would give in to the melancholy that engulfed him regularly. The war was over, and he was no good to the navy with only half an arm. London was filled with soldiers and sailors, and wages were low for the few jobs to be found. It had taken very hard work, stretching every farthing to its limit, to survive the few years following Waterloo, and if not for *Fifty Ways to Sin* suddenly dropping into their laps, Bathsheba wasn't sure they would have survived.

But that long shared adversity, when it seemed she and Danny only had each other, had bound the siblings together. Just as Danny had worried she was making a mistake by breaking off her engagement with Henry the grocer, he would be violently alarmed if she disappeared for the night. If he ever discovered Liam was involved, Bathsheba didn't doubt that her brother would call him out. Therefore, as little as she liked lying to Danny, she would have to do it, and do it well.

She concocted a story: her childhood friend Estella, who used to live near them but who had recently removed to a farm on the outskirts of London, had invited her to visit— perhaps to help with a sick child. If Danny ever asked Estella, Bathsheba knew her friend would support her story, but fortunately Danny did not like Estella much and was unlikely to seek her out. Of course, if she were going to Estella, she would likely leave early in the day, while Liam had never sent a carriage for her before eight in the evening. It was a vexing problem, and Bathsheba felt more than a little frustration that she couldn't come and go as she pleased.

She was still debating when Danny solved it for her. "I'll be away tomorrow evening," he told her at dinner the day before Liam's week was up.

"Oh?" Her pulse leapt, but she tried to maintain her calm. "Business?" Danny had built up a business printing select commissions, having discreetly put his name around after the runaway success of *Fifty Ways to Sin*. Thanks to that increased business—and Bathsheba's secret income from *Lady X*—they were comfortable again, but poverty was too recent a memory for her to feel secure.

"Yes."

"That's good," she said, immediately wondering if she could use this to her advantage.

Danny was pushing his fish around his plate. "It's a good distance from town. I've been invited to dinner, and then to stay the night."

Her mouth dropped open at this gift from God. "You have?"

It almost looked like her brother was blushing. "The job is a gentleman's private library, Mr. Edmund Brown. He was a collector, and it was discovered in some disarray when he died last year. Some texts are old and must be reprinted, and most require binding. The family solicitor engaged me to bind a few, and Mr. Brown's widow was pleased enough with my work to offer me the rest of the library. It's a healthy commission, but will take a great deal of time. The dinner invitation is so that we may spend the day and evening assessing the scope of it."

"Well, it sounds like you should take it, including staying

the night if necessary." She smiled, her heart thudding fast inside her chest.

"Yes!" He beamed at her in relief. "I shall. You won't be worried to be alone?"

Bathsheba waved one hand. "Of course not. Where is it?"

"Greenwich. I may need to spend plenty of time there, as many books are too fragile to be transported to London and back."

Greenwich—excellent. That would make it so much easier for her to say she was going to visit a friend and give the servants the night free tomorrow. Her stomach tightened at the realization that she was actually going to do this, slip away like a wanton and spend the night with Liam.

She said good-bye to her brother in the morning. He was clearly eager to be off, barely pausing to give her a wave before he disappeared into the traffic at the end of the street. Bathsheba closed the door and looked at the clock. Barely half past seven. She had an entire day to prepare, and she needed every moment of it.

By eight o'clock that evening, she had had time to make daring decisions, time to talk herself out of them, time to fret, and time to recover her bravado. Mary had gone home an hour earlier, pleased to have an extra evening free, and Bathsheba was able to prepare in solitude. The whole evening felt unreal, but never more so than when she caught a glimpse of herself in the mirror. She looked a complete stranger to her own eyes.

But that was appropriate; she was different inside as well. She had thought Liam would teach her about seduction, but she'd never guessed he would teach her about herself. After two nights in his arms, not to mention all the days in between when she daydreamed of making him fall in love with her, she was learning that she was more sensual and lustful than expected. His touch was branded on her skin, and the slightest touch of her own hands seemed to rouse all the hunger he had awoken within her. She had only asked him for seduction and pleasure, but it was impossible to deny that she wanted more—and she was willing to make a bold play in pursuit of it.

When the coachman rapped at her door she breathed a sigh of relief. Even though she'd never sent Liam word that she wasn't coming, part of her had feared he wouldn't send the coach after all. She put out the last lamp and locked the door behind her, keeping her cloak close around her against the cool night air. The coachman took her small valise and helped her into the carriage as usual, and then she was off, headed toward what felt like a turning point in her life.

Chapter Nine

This time the door of the cottage was closed, although light glowed in the windows. Bathsheba's heart lurched into her throat as the carriage rolled down the narrow drive toward that closed door. Sudden doubt assaulted her. What if she had mistaken the matter? She'd assumed, because he sent the carriage, that Liam wanted her to come tonight—but if he were still angry from their last meeting and intended something different—

Too late. There was no time to change her plan. The vehicle stopped and the driver opened the door. Clutching her cloak in one hand, she stepped down and took her valise before turning to the door. Her shoes crunched on the gravel, and her breathing seemed just as loud.

The door opened and she stopped in her tracks. Liam gazed at her, his expression aloof. He was dressed as informally as before, the silk banyan over his trousers and shirt, but there was no welcome in his eyes.

"Good evening," she said.

He gave a short nod and held the door for her. Bathsheba stepped inside and let him take her valise. In the moment his back was turned to close the door and set the bag down, she untied her cloak and let it fall. Liam turned and froze.

"You said to wear nothing at all, but I thought this was quite fetching," she said, holding her shoulders stiffly back as his gaze slid over her. She wore a nightdress, but one unlike anything else she'd ever owned. It was made of the sheerest, finest cotton lawn, with slender straps over her shoulders, a fitted bodice more meant to push up and display her breasts than conceal them, and a flowing skirt that was slit past her knees in front. It was virtually transparent and had cost more than she would have spent in a month on the butcher bill, but standing there, just shy of naked with her hair streaming loose down her back as Liam stared in open hunger, Bathsheba thought it was worth it.

"Lovely," he said at last. He stepped up close, so close she faltered a step backward to keep her balance. Defiantly she raised her gaze to meet his. The remote closed look had gone from his face. "And convenient," he whispered, trailing his fingertips down her bare arms. Bathsheba shivered. His fingers encircled her wrists as he pressed her back against the wall.

She had resolved not to question anything he did tonight. Let him teach her what he would. He knew her body better than she did, it seemed, and she didn't want the affair to end—not yet, not ever. If it made her a coward or weak, she had already admitted that: she was weak where he was concerned. And for tonight, at least, she wouldn't fight it.

He pinned her hands above her head with one hand and let his other hand run down her body. He cupped her breast, scraping his nail over her nipple, already erect. She shivered, and a faint, wicked smile touched his lips. Down her ribs, over her hips his hand went, drawing up the hem of her nightdress until it was bunched around her waist. He bent his knees, and for a startled moment she thought he meant to use his mouth again, making her stand this time, but instead he caught her knee and lifted it up, up, up until she was dependent on him to stay upright.

He released her hands. "Hold on to my shoulders," he commanded, his voice rough and low. "That's it," he whispered as she clutched at him. Her knee still hooked over his arm, he reached between her spread legs and touched her.

Bathsheba jolted. He pressed against her, his weight holding her to the wall as his fingers played on her exposed center. She had to gulp for breath; unlike other times he wasn't easing her along but pushing her, pulling her, driving her onward. "Liam," she gasped, her hips jerking involuntarily. "Wait—"

"Stop?" He went still, and a spasm of longing shook her. Without a word she shook her head. He resumed, resting his cheek against her temple and murmuring that she should scream as loudly as she pleased, there was no one to hear but him, and he *wanted* to make her scream, he wouldn't stop until she did, he knew how to make her come so hard she wouldn't be able to stop herself—

Panting, her head buzzing, Bathsheba shook in his grip, feeling her climax building with frightening speed. He had pinned her open and defenseless to his wicked fingers but she wouldn't have stopped him for the world. If he stopped she would have fallen to her knees to beg, so long as he gave her what her body wanted—*needed*—

It hit her like a wave. She arched her neck and gave a long, thin cry of release. Liam adjusted his hold on her, yanked at his trousers, and then her cry was cut short as he thrust inside her, hard and deep and so thick, she gasped in astonishment. "Go on," he growled, and thrust again.

Again. Bathsheba saw stars even before he resumed that firm insistent stroke on what felt like the nexus of every nerve in her body. Another wave slammed into her, knocking her breathless, and another. He was panting, too, and yanked his arm from under her leg to curl around her shoulders as he drove into her, harder and faster until she was clinging to him with arms and legs and oblivious to anything but the scorching pleasure of his body moving with hers.

On the last ripple of climax, Liam swore violently under his breath, and slammed her against the wall one last time, holding himself deep within her. Wrung out and dazed, Bathsheba could only hold on and wonder what had happened.

After a moment, he lifted his head. "Brisk and efficient," he whispered, his words hot on her ear. "As you wished." She was too weak to do more than give a slight nod of acknowledgment. "Do you want lesson three now, to compare?" he added, with a swipe of his tongue on the sensitive skin beneath her ear.

Oh God. Lesson three. More pleasure. More of Liam. He was still inside her, remarkably big. He had invaded and conquered her, almost without a word, and even though she would never admit it aloud, he had stolen her heart as well. Again she gave a slight nod.

He stepped away, disengaging from her before he fastened a button on his trousers, then to her surprise he caught her up in his arms.

Liam carried her up the stairs to his bedroom. The way she curled her arms around his neck and rested her cheek against his chest drove the final stake into his heart. He was mad for this woman. It was like she'd been made for him. His last resistance, his last doubt, had disintegrated when she took off her cloak to reveal a transparent nightdress that would have incited riots. Her breasts, so pert and perfect; her soft belly and round hips; the dark curls at the apex of her thighs. And her long silky hair, falling over his arm. She might only want him for what he could give her in bed, but he could build on that until she agreed with him: they were meant for each other.

He set her down on the thick carpet in front of the fireplace and stripped off his clothes. Her nightdress was barely clothing at all, so he left it on for the moment. Bathsheba watched him, her gaze fascinated but somehow vulnerable.

"No questions tonight?" he asked.

She shook her head. "No. Whatever you want to teach me, I want to learn. Your way has been better than anything I could have asked for."

His heart jumped. That was promising. "I am glad it met your hopes."

Something flickered in her eyes. "You must know it has surpassed every one of my hopes."

Do you know it has only raised mine? He didn't say it, not yet. He wanted to give her one last lesson in pleasure before he broached the topic that had bedeviled him all week. If she didn't like his proposal, at least he would have this night with her.

"Come here." He reached for her hand, then tugged her closer. He folded his arms around her, her back to his chest, and took a long inhale with his face against her lavender-scented hair. When he prepared the room, before he'd been fully confident she would arrive, he had lit a pair of lamps. Now he wished he'd lit every lamp in the house and placed them all in this room so he could see every fleeting expression that dashed across her face, every inch of her body as he made her his. "I'm sorry," he breathed. "For what happened downstairs."

She stiffened. "There is no need—"

"You dropped the cloak and blew apart my plans." He slid one finger under the strap of her wispy-thin nightdress and eased it down her shoulder. "This is bewitching."

The tension melted from her shoulders. "Do you like it? Better than my brown velvet or green cotton?"

"Much better." He applied his mouth to the slope of her bare shoulder, letting his finger drift down to her breast. The gauzy cloth did nothing to obscure how rosy and pert her nipple was. "You should patronize that modiste for your entire wardrobe."

"Oh my." Her laugh was shaky and more like a sigh of pleasure as his palm cupped her breast, his thumb teasing the peak. "I could never afford Madame Follette's for everything . . ."

"It would be worth it." He slipped the other strap down and undid the ribbon holding the bodice closed. Another tug and the ribbon that ran beneath her breasts came loose, letting the garment slide down her body to puddle around her feet.

He urged her down onto her knees, then onto hands and knees. Her head fell forward as he ran his palms over her back, smoothing over the firm plumpness of her hips. This time he lingered over her, testing and teasing in search of every sensitive spot on her body. He wanted to know every inch of her and discover every little thing that made her sigh. This was Bathsheba, who never hesitated to tell him exactly what she thought, whose mind worked the same way his did, and whose passions ran as hot as his.

And now she was in his bedroom, his conquest, his conqueror, his equal.

Liam didn't believe in luck; luck was the word lazy people used when hard effort and preparation finally paid off. It hadn't been luck that saved the *Intelligencer* when he almost went bankrupt, it was a wise choice of investors—namely Arthur Wilde, who left his twelve percent share to his widow Madeline. It hadn't been luck that made his subscriptions grow after Madeline began writing a gossip column for the newspaper, it was the deliberate cultivation of mystery around the anonymous but highborn columnist who reported the most scandalous, choicest gossip in London. It wasn't luck that made his side business printing novels and poetry enormously profitable, it was a clear-eyed evaluation of the demand for the sort of books that Bathsheba wrote.

But he didn't have a good explanation for *this*. What had made Bathsheba bring her proposition to him? For all that he'd been shocked by it, he'd known from the start that he didn't want her turning to someone else: *don't you dare,* he'd said when she suggested it. He could tell himself he was concerned for her safety and her reputation, but there was more; he didn't want her to be like this with someone else. Until that moment she had kept their relationship cordial and professional, and he had been satisfied with that—but the moment the prospect of *more* was dangled in front of him, Liam snatched it. Had he wanted her all along? Or had he been blind? He didn't know. But now that he did see quite clearly, he didn't want it to end.

Even though he knew what she liked already, he took his time, making her writhe and arch beneath his hands and mouth. He turned her over onto the floor and she spread herself before him like a feast, inviting him to gorge himself on her pale skin and pink nipples and silky curls. Her dark eyes glowed with desire and he realized she was lovely—

not as most in London thought of beauty, but the way he did. Her intelligence had won his respect, her talent won his admiration. Her dry humor made him laugh. Perhaps he shouldn't feel any astonishment that he was falling in love; rather, he should wonder why he hadn't fallen sooner.

If Bathsheba had thought lessons one and two were satisfying, she was rapidly realizing that Liam hadn't shown her everything, not by half. This night, knowing they had hours, he seemed bent on destroying whatever resistance her heart had left. His hands began so gently, roving over her body as if smoothing the way for his mouth. But the hard, rapid coupling against the wall downstairs had been so erotic, so needy, her body was already humming with anticipation. "Harder," she whispered to him, and he responded. "Faster," she moaned to him, and he complied. *Take me,* she begged silently as he pulled her toward ecstasy. *I'm yours if only you can love me.*

She was crying, shaking, on the verge of eruption, when he pulled away from her. Roughly he spread her knees wide, and thrust home. Instinctively her body tightened around him, and his face grew fierce. Deliberately he hiked her knees up, until she curled her legs around his waist, and then he planted one hand behind each of her shoulders. His first thrust made her clutch at his arms. The second made her back arch; he angled his hips so that every invasion raked across the most sensitive nerve endings in her body. At the first rush of climax she bit back a scream and squeezed her eyes shut, her breath catching in anticipation.

"No," he rasped. "Look at me." His gray gaze bored into her, pupils dilated. His hair swung around his face as he moved.

Bathsheba started to shake. She was coming, her climax boiling up inside her, from her toes through her thighs through her belly until it seemed to seize her lungs. Her eyes widened as it broke; Liam's blazing gaze had mesmerized her until she couldn't blink or look away.

"Yes," he growled, pumping hard. "Yes—like that—" He ducked his head and kissed her as he drove himself so deep inside her, Bathsheba thought it might tear her apart. But then his tongue was in her mouth, and she strained against him, kissing him back, her trembling arms around his neck as he reached his own release. When he finally lifted his head, she gasped for air, feeling as if she hadn't taken a breath in minutes.

"You . . . you never kissed me before," she said faintly, her heart still racing.

"My mistake," he whispered, brushing his lips against hers before settling in for another long, deep kiss that scattered what little sense she had left.

He helped her off the floor eventually and carried her to bed, tucking her snugly against him. Bathsheba sank into the fine linens and indulged in a moment of fantasy. *I never imagined these lessons in seduction would take such a turn,* he said in her imagination. *Bathsheba, I don't want this to end . . . I love you . . .* No matter how frequently and firmly she had told herself that Liam was only taking what she offered, that men could enjoy a vigorous romp in bed . . . or on a sofa or on a chaise . . . and not develop any finer feelings for the woman involved, her wayward heart persisted in trying to spin straw into gold.

He lingered over her pleasure, saying he wanted to learn her and let her learn him.

He canceled a dinner engagement to be with her.

He wanted her to stay all night.

He kissed her.

"You were right," she murmured.

"Oh?" He sounded amused. "How noble of you to admit it."

"Of course I would admit it," she protested, then added tartly, "once you proved your point, naturally."

He laughed, a low relaxed sound. His fingers were combing idly through her hair, and she could have sighed aloud at how like a *lover* it was. "Which point?"

She hesitated. Her cheek was against his shoulder, his arm beneath her head. "Your way was superior."

His fingers slowed, then resumed stroking her hair. "I'm delighted you agreed to try it."

How could she not? Bathsheba felt the end of their interlude approaching; this would likely be the last night. Her fingers curled into a fist against his bare chest, where she could feel the steady thump of his heart, still rapid after their lovemaking.

But it didn't beat for her.

"Why did you want me to stay?" she asked to divert her mind from that. It would spoil the whole night, this lone magical night she had with him.

His fingers paused. "Because," he finally said, very slowly, "seduction is more than the physical act, whether that act be 'brisk and efficient' or leisurely and thorough. I felt you deserved the full range."

"Then, there will be more tonight?" She honestly didn't know what else he could mean to teach her. Her limbs already were like jelly and she felt the most blissful exhaustion of her life.

Liam was quiet for a long moment. He tipped up her chin until she met his gaze. She had never seen that expression in his eyes before—searching, almost wary, and full of urgency. "Do you not want more?"

Her face burned. She did—she wanted so much more, the words themselves were too big to speak. For a moment the question seemed to burn in the air, the fulcrum on which her life might turn. She had admired Liam—wanted Liam—from the start, but now she'd gone and fallen hopelessly in love with him. If she told him . . .

"I planned on an entire night," he added. "The carriage won't return for you until morning."

She blushed, relieved that he'd spoken before she could blurt out her adoration. He referred only to tonight—that answer was easier. "Yes."

Chapter Ten

She woke in the night, disoriented and cold. For a moment Bathsheba lay still in alarmed confusion; the blankets had fallen off, but why was she naked? She groped for the covers and encountered Liam's bare chest.

She went still, her fingers still brushing his skin. He was warm and firm and so male. Her *ideal* male. She had expected a night of lovemaking, but he'd given her more: not just physical pleasure but emotional pleasure as well. Bathsheba didn't have many close friends. The trials of daily life, coupled with the swings in her fortunes, had left little time for friends. At times she wondered if she even knew how to let down her guard with others. It was strange, then, how she felt so at ease with Liam.

Bathsheba laid her hand against his chest and felt the steady thump of his heart. His heart might not be hers, but she had learned to take what life offered her. And if this interlude with Liam was all she got, she would save up every moment in her memory.

He stirred at her touch. "Too early," he muttered, reaching for her. Bathsheba let him draw her close and tug the blankets over both of them.

"It's almost dawn," she whispered.

His lips brushed the back of her neck. "Almost doesn't

count."

She smiled. "It's a long drive back to London. I dare not linger."

"You'll be home before the street lamps are put out, even if you lie here another hour."

"Is that so?" He growled a sleepy affirmation. Outside the window a thrush called, the sound sweet and clear in the night. One didn't hear that in Totman Street. "Why do you live so far from town?" she asked on impulse.

He shifted, settling her more comfortably against him. His voice was a drowsy rumble, but he answered readily. "It's quiet here. My father told me land was the best investment. And if I lived in London my mother would come to call on me all the time, which would be untenable. All in all, it's perfect."

"You bought this house to avoid your mother?"

He grunted. "Of course not. I dine with her every Sunday, discuss the latest gossip, endure my brother's company—and then I leave. If she came to call at my home, manners would prevent me from leaving."

Bathsheba's shoulders shook with silent laughter. "I don't believe you!"

"No?" He kissed her neck. "Perhaps you're right. My manners aren't fine enough to keep me from leaving. But my mother is persistent; odds are she would follow, even if I claimed the *Intelligencer* was burning to the ground at that moment. I would know no peace."

He dined with his mother every Sunday. Bathsheba's mother had died nearly ten years ago. A wistful smile curved her lips, and she was glad he couldn't see it. "So you fled."

"For my own preservation," he agreed. "It took me twenty years to realize it, but my mother always gets her way. She looks harmless and sweet, but she's relentless. Kings would quail before her. My brother and I had no chance, but, being by far the cleverer of us, I escaped to St. John's Wood."

Her smile faded. "Danny used to say *I* was relentless," she said in a low voice. "When he came home from the war."

"I expect if you were, it was for his own good."

"It was," she agreed. "He needed it. But I felt like an awful scold." She half turned her head. "I had to be, to save us both from being cast on the parish or thrown into the Fleet."

"And you did, so you have nothing to regret."

"Perhaps." She hesitated. "I worried over what my parents would think. My mother would have wanted me to marry Henry the grocer, no matter how cold the marriage would have been. He's a good man, you know, and it would have provided security."

His arms tightened around her. "Rubbish. She would have wanted you to sell yourself into marital servitude? Even if she did, you had every right to reject that for yourself."

"You think so?"

"Of course," he said, sounding mildly surprised. "Why shouldn't you? It is your life; it was your decision. If I'd followed what my father wanted me to do, I would be adding up columns in the bank office, with my brain withered away to nothing."

Her eyes widened. "A banker?"

"Noxious, isn't it?" His laugh rumbled deep in his chest. "I fled from the prospect as if the hangman were after me. But I do confess, if the *Intelligencer* hadn't trafficked in so much gossip—my mother's fascination—I'm sure she would have badgered me to follow his example. So in a way, I fended off both of them."

She turned over and went up on her elbows to look down at him. The steel gray of dawn gave just enough light for her to make out his features, relaxed and so handsome, it made her chest hurt. "I don't believe you."

"It's true." He gave a lazy grin. "How dare you impugn my honesty."

"No!" She laughed and shook her head. "I don't believe you were ever terrified or intimidated by your mother. You're impervious. You do exactly as you wish, and don't care a fig for anyone's opinion of you."

"You think not?" His grin lingered, but his gaze was more thoughtful. "Everyone cares for someone else's opinion—even if only one person's. No one is impervious."

"You give every appearance of it," she told him.

"Well." He pulled her against him. "Let me disabuse you of that notion." He rolled over her, nuzzling her neck until she laughed, and then there was no more conversation.

He walked her to the carriage an hour later. It was early, the sky pale gold and the ground dewy. The roses were in bloom, and in the brief moment when Liam turned to hand her valise to the coachman, Bathsheba thought it was the most perfect day of all time. On impulse, she flung her arms around Liam's neck when he turned back to her.

"Thank you," she breathed.

He caught her, his hands on her back. "For what, specifically?"

She kissed him. "For everything," she said softly. "It was all I hoped for and more." Bathsheba gave a tremulous smile. "You fulfilled our bargain perfectly," she said, reminding herself that this was important to clarify.

"Our bargain," he echoed, suddenly serious. "Bathsheba, that bargain—"

A shout made them both start. A horse was trotting down the lane toward them, a gentleman in tweed on his back. Liam swore under his breath as Bathsheba froze. Her heart kicked painfully hard; she didn't want anyone to see her leaving Liam's house at dawn, no doubt looking as though she'd spent the night in debauched pleasure.

"Damn it," said Liam under his breath. He yanked open the carriage door. "You'd better go."

She yanked up the hood of her cloak. "Yes." She was already jumping in, keeping her head down. "Good-bye."

He didn't even reply, merely closed the carriage door and barked at the coachman to drive. Bathsheba huddled well away from the window, keeping her face hidden. The rider openly stared as the carriage passed him, but she turned away, holding her breath until the carriage was well past him.

Who had come to call on Liam so early in the morning? Had he seen her well enough to identify her? And by all the saints, could he be trusted not to spread rumors that would ruin her?

Liam forced himself to keep his eyes on his brother and not on the carriage carrying Bathsheba away. He wanted to curse in frustration at the timing of the interruption, spoiling the moment when he was about to confess to Bathsheba that he'd stopped thinking of that bloody bargain a long time ago. He should have told her last night, but like a coward he'd put it off. In the morning, he'd told himself, he would tell her, and even hint that his heart was engaged. Liam had never told a woman he loved her, and it had seemed like a sound plan to work toward that moment gradually.

But somehow all the hours of the night had sped by, with Bathsheba in his bed, in his arms, burrowing into his very soul. And now she was gone, before he managed to find the right moment to speak, and his rotter of a brother was here, which did nothing to help his temper.

"What do you want, Angus?"

His brother swung off his horse, his face alive with interest. "Is that the woman who threw herself at you? The one who tossed up her own skirts for you?"

"None of your affair," Liam bit out. "What do you want?"

Angus swiveled on one heel to peer after the departing carriage, then back. "It was, wasn't it? Quite the devil, aren't you?" Grinning like a fiend, he punched Liam in the shoulder. "I didn't get a good look, but she appeared a fetching little woman." He made a show of looking Liam up and down. "And I see you're just out of bed, so she must have many charms!"

Liam glared at him. He'd dressed quickly and haphazardly, not intending to see or be seen by anyone except Bathsheba. "If you rode out here at dawn trying to catch me in an assignation—"

"If I did, then it worked!" Angus roared with laughter. "No, I was entirely sure you were lying about that and had no thought you'd be rushing her out the door. Is she married? You'd better hope her husband's a careless fellow, or too big a fool to notice his wife is letting you plow her field."

Liam had his brother's cravat in his hand before the last

word. "Stop there," he snarled. "Not one bloody word to anyone about her, do you hear me?"

Angus blinked, shocked, but still enjoying Liam's anger too much. "Why should I? It's not my place to spoil your *amour...*" He paused, looking sly. "Although you'd better be more discreet about it, if you want to keep her a secret."

"Perhaps I'll hire guards to patrol my property and shoot anyone who trespasses." He shoved Angus away and turned toward the house. "Go away."

"But I came to tell you John Winston is leading a shooting party on the heath today," Angus said, dogging his heels. "He spied a flock of geese. Will you come, or have you had too much sport today?"

Liam stopped, not needing to turn around to know Angus wore a wide, toothy grin. "No."

"Worn you to a nub, has she?" Angus chortled again. "Drained you dry? I confess, my curiosity about this woman grows and grows."

"And as is so often the case, you are destined to remain ignorant." Liam paused in the doorway. "And if you tell Winston aught of her, you'll regret it."

Something in his tone must have finally penetrated his brother's glee. The smug look faded from Angus's face. "What—you don't say—"

"If you gossip about my personal affairs, I beg you to remember I own a newspaper."

Angus drew up in affront. "There's no call for that. Have I got it wrong? Have you got a wealthy widow on the line, being reeled in one bedroom romp at a time?"

Liam stared at him. "No wonder you're a banker. You've got bollocks for brains."

A cunning smile returned to his brother's face. "No? A Covent Garden whore? Don't say it—an aspiring newspaper writer, looking to see her name in print?"

He took a deep breath and let it out, counting to twenty as he did so. "Angus," he said, "Go home. Tell Winston I've no desire to go shooting today. Then pay a call upon Miss Lachlan and tell her you're going out of your wits without her. Get down on your knee and beg her to end her mourning early and set a date for the wedding. Then you'll have your own *amour* to entertain you." He spat out the word *amour* with disdain.

"I say." Angus looked offended. "There's no reason to bring her into this—"

"If you want to pick apart my romantic life, I'm perfectly capable of returning the favor."

His brother's eyes narrowed. "Quite defensive." He cocked his head in the direction of the long-since departed carriage. "She's not a whore, is she, nor some married lady looking for a spot of fun."

Liam was quiet for a minute. Bathsheba was none of that, nor was she any of the other things Angus had suggested. She was his friend, his partner, his lover—all by her own initiative. That had been niggling at him for a while, and finally here and now it condensed. It was time for *him* to take some initiative, if he wanted more. "No."

Slowly Angus shook his head. The humor had fled from his face and he looked almost pitying. "Then you're done for, lad. As your older and much wiser brother, I regret to inform you that the only way that sort of affair can end well is if you marry her."

Chapter Eleven

For several days Bathsheba pondered the etiquette of ending an affair.

On one hand, since it had been essentially a business arrangement between them, perhaps she ought to send a note of thanks. But on the other hand, her mind went completely blank at the thought of writing anything that came close to conveying her feelings about the nights spent with Liam. She considered writing to remind him of their mutual vow of discretion, but worried that would be insulting and pointless. If he had decided to tell his friends, her caution would mean little to him. Indecision bedeviled her until so much time had passed, it would seem stranger to send a letter than not to, so she wrote nothing, and instantly began worrying that it was a mistake.

She had no excuse or reason to see Liam. She returned to work on her next story, the words flowing smoothly, but somehow with far less delight than before. Her days settled back into an ordinary rhythm, the same as always and yet somehow utterly different. Danny's work in Greenwich was demanding, and he was gone more often than he was home. Even when he was home he spent most of his time printing or at the bindery. On the rare nights they dined together, he was very reluctant to talk about his client.

Bathsheba put together that the client was a wealthy widow, quite demanding and exacting, and it caused her a pang of worry that her brother was taking on such onerous work to provide for them. Perhaps she ought to tell him about *Lady X*. The stories had earned her a nice sum . . . but hardly enough to put all their financial worries to rest. And if Danny knew what she had done in the interest of research, he would be furious.

She was plodding through a scene one morning when her maid tapped at the door. "Mr. MacGregor to see you, ma'am," said Mary.

Bathsheba's pen skittered across the paper, leaving a blotchy trail of ink behind it. What was he doing here? Why would he come? Merciful heavens, what if Danny came home?

Trying to still the trembling of her fingers, she put the pen down and blotted all that wasted ink. "I'll be right down," she told her maid. "Show him into the parlor."

Mary disappeared and Bathsheba folded her hands tightly in her lap. She had worked with Liam for the better part of a year now, and not once had he come to her home. They communicated via penny post or her visits to his office, which was more convenient for both of them. He was always at the *Intelligencer,* after all. And never had she detected the slightest interest on Liam's part in calling upon her at home.

As if they were lovers.

As if they were . . . more.

She rose from her chair and smoothed a hand over her head. Her hair was pinned into the soft chignon Mary had grown adept at arranging. It was just as practical as the braided knot, but looser. Her dress was a new one, raspberry-colored with a delicate trail of embroidery at the neckline. Even though it had been ridiculous to spend money on a new dress she didn't need, Bathsheba liked it. She felt almost handsome in it, and every time the pink skirt swished around her, she remembered Liam saying she should wear colors. Now she twitched that soft, pretty skirt into place, put her shoulders back, and went down the stairs to the parlor.

Mary had left the door open, and late morning sun spilled through the doorway. Bathsheba's steps slowed as she crossed the hall and her heart sped up. With a deep breath, she walked into the room. "Good morning. What a surprise."

He turned. After three weeks of separation, it was like seeing him for the first time, tall and lean, dark hair ruffled as if he'd pushed his hand through it. The force of attraction nearly bowled her over, even now, and she surreptitiously placed one hand on the door to steady herself.

"Good morning, Bathsheba." He paused. "You look well."

She had to clear her throat; a lump had formed at the sound of his voice. With a quick breath—chiding herself for being emotionally unbalanced—she closed the door and came into the room. "Won't you sit down?"

He took the small sofa opposite her. The Crawford parlor had seen better days, but it had also seen far worse. It didn't have the eccentric charm or the secluded quiet of Liam's house in St. John's Wood. Bathsheba was irrationally aware of this as she perched on the edge of the armchair.

"How have you been?" Liam asked, his gaze intent upon her.

"Very well, thank you." She pressed her hands into the

fabric of her skirt to keep from fidgeting. "You?"

His mouth quirked. "Perfectly well." He hesitated. "I've not received pages from you, and wondered when I may expect them. It's been several weeks since the last story was published. I've been receiving queries."

"Oh." This was good news, and yet her heart seemed to drop from her throat all the way to her shoes. He'd come on business. She tried to rally a pleased expression. "How wonderful that it's wanted. I should have something by next week."

"Excellent," he said with a quick smile. "I had begun to fear—" He coughed. "That is, I'm relieved you're working as usual."

"Mmm-hmm." She rubbed her hands back and forth, her smile stiff. *As usual.* As usual, she pictured Liam's handsome face on every hero she wrote. As usual, she thought of him every night when she retired to her quiet bed, and wondered if he had a new lover.

"I also worried . . ." His gaze dipped momentarily to her midsection. "You've not suffered any . . . unease?"

She blushed deep red. Had she conceived a child, he meant. She had wondered if she might, for a few days after their glorious night together, but that had soon been put to rest. Some tiny, unreasonable part of her had dwelt on the prospect with longing. Her heart yearned for Liam's child in her arms, a little hand in hers, a lifelong reminder of her one taste of sensual bliss with the man she loved. She might never have another chance to be a mother, and it had taken her off guard how appealing it suddenly seemed.

But she also knew it would be a terrible thing for that child, to be illegitimate and possibly unwanted by his father, so when her monthly courses arrived on schedule, she told herself it was for the best.

"None," she assured him.

"Ah." His face was inscrutable. She couldn't tell if his response was relieved or disappointed. Perhaps he'd merely had his curiosity satisfied.

"I would have notified you if so," she added.

"Of course." He glanced at the door. "I trust it remains our secret?"

She blushed again. "Danny doesn't know, and never will."

"Are you . . ." Liam seemed to be choosing every word with great care. "He would not beat you if he knew, would he?"

Bathsheba blinked. If her brother would beat anyone, it would be Liam. "No. I'm sure not."

"But he would be displeased?" Liam persisted, his voice low. "You were so adamant that he not know about *Lady X*, I couldn't help but wonder if he would take it badly if he knew about us."

She bit her lip. "Danny would not be pleased," she admitted. "He believes himself responsible for me, even though I've told him many times he mustn't feel so."

"I see." Liam looked at the floor. "Would he be displeased on principle, or because I was the man?"

What was he after? Suddenly wary, she tried to parse his question. "Both, I imagine," she said cautiously. "He would not like me taking a—a lover, and as he knows you, I suspect he would view it as a sort of betrayal. He would likely have wanted you to refuse my entreaty and then perhaps even tell him what I'd done, so he could put a stop to it." Liam's eyes flashed, and she stopped. "But he'll never know," she promised quickly. "Not from my lips, and I told no one at all. Only your coachman knows . . . and the man who called upon you that last morning . . ."

Her voice trailed off questioningly. She'd suffered a thousand pangs of curiosity and dread over that man.

Now Liam looked awkward. "That was my brother Angus. He was neither expected nor welcome. I extracted his promise not to say a word, and he's got no idea who you are."

"Oh." She let out her breath in relief.

"Bathsheba, I think you ought to tell your brother," said Liam. She froze, eyes wide. "About *Lady X*. Your sales have been strong, steadily growing. I know you wished to keep it secret in case things did not go well, but they unquestionably *are* going well. You plan to keep writing, don't you?"

"Well—yes, but—"

"Daniel didn't disapprove of you working on *Fifty Ways to Sin*. He knew you read it, even edited some issues," Liam went on. "I think you do him wrong to believe he would view it as indecency."

Her mouth was hanging open. "I never said that—"

"Then why don't you tell him?" Liam edged forward. "You're succeeding. You think he worries about providing for you, but you're providing for yourself. Why do you hide this from him?"

"Because it's not enough," she said before she could think better of it. Liam sat back, brows raised. Bathsheba sighed. "The money I've saved . . . It's not enough to show him and say, there—you needn't worry about providing for us."

"When will it be?"

She raised her hands and let them fall helplessly. "I don't know. Perhaps never. It's not reliable like an annuity, you know."

"So you intend to keep it secret forever?"

"I don't know," she said again.

"Is it only about the money?" There was an underlying urgency in his question that unsettled her. Why did it matter to Liam if Danny knew what she was doing? And why did she not have any answer about telling her brother? Her small savings was not trivial, and even if it would never be enough for her to feel completely secure, it would surely give Danny some comfort to know she had it. But she hadn't told him.

"Mostly," she muttered.

Liam was quiet for a moment. "Is it because you fear it would reveal your deepest desires, and you're ashamed of having them?" Bathsheba sucked in her breath indignantly. "Or is it because you're afraid of pursuing them, so much that you'd rather give up all hope of gaining them?"

"What does that mean?" she demanded, furious.

"You'd rather lie to your brother for the rest of your life to keep him from knowing you write successful stories. You'd rather spend the rest of your life minding his house and protecting him than strike out after something that brings you pleasure."

"I wonder what you mean by that," she retorted. "I *did* strike out after pleasure. But now that's done and I must live my life"

"So tamely and nervously?" he persisted. "Sneaking around any time you want to have a word about your writing. Pretending he's the only source of support you've got."

Sneaking around. Bathsheba stared at him. "Sneaking around to see you, do you mean?"

Liam's mouth firmed into a flat line. He said nothing.

She drew a deep breath. "If I told Danny, you think it would make me more independent, more daring. I could go out whenever I chose, and spend the night where I wished. Is that it? Do you want to carry on as we were?"

His eyes flashed. "You make it sound so craven. I didn't advocate telling Daniel in the hopes of prolonging our affair. I thought you wanted to be independent, and not have to lie to him about where you are going. Don't you want to have a life of your own?"

"I do have a life of my own," she protested. "Perhaps not the life you would choose, but it's the one I've chosen."

"But if you weren't hiding—"

"Then what?" She shook her head. "I have to think of Danny, too."

"He's a grown man," Liam pointed out. "He could make do without you."

"Yes, but what would *I* do?" Bathsheba asked before she could stop herself.

Liam opened his mouth, and then he went still, as if frozen in mid-thought. The silence stretched taut. For a wild second she hoped he would say, *elope with me.* Because she would. For Liam, for his love, she would leave Danny without a qualm. All he had to do was say one word . . .

But that was unlikely, and sure enough he didn't say it. After a long pause, during which he seemed to struggle with some inner decision, he gave a nod. "Very well. As you say, it is your life to choose. I should be going." They both rose and Liam bowed. "Oh yes—" He clapped one hand to his side as if just remembering. "You forgot this," he said with a hint of his usual wry smile. He drew out her reticule from his coat pocket. "Good day, Miss Crawford."

She bobbed a slight curtsey and he left her standing there with the reticule in her hands. The front door closed behind him and she flinched, knowing it was probably the last time. Slowly she sank back into her chair. Was he right?

Ought she to tell Danny—not just about *Lady X*, but about her desire to have a lover? The only reason she could see for Liam's bewildering insistence that she drop the secrecy was that he wanted to continue their affair, which made her heart take a leap even as her mind protested. If three nights had left such a deep mark on her, what might three months—three years—do to her?

Bathsheba was still sitting there, deeply uncertain, when the front door opened again, and there came the sound of Danny's familiar tread in the hall. A moment later he was in the doorway. "Bathsheba! Could I have a word?"

"Of course," she said as he came in and took Liam's seat. "Are you well? I didn't expect you so early."

He nodded. "Perfectly well. I've got something to tell you, which I hope will come as happy news."

"Oh." She tensed. Danny looked braced for a bad reaction, which put her on guard. What had he done?

"This job in Greenwich has been very profitable," he said. "I told you Mrs. Brown engaged me to repair her late husband's library. It happened to include a number of—er—erotic books, of which I'm sure the lady was ignorant at the start." He went pink. "Catherine—Mrs. Brown, I mean—and I spent a great deal of time together, sorting out which books ought to be restored and which ought to be sold or disposed of." He cleared his throat, looking young and awkward for a moment, and in a flash Bathsheba knew what her brother was going to say. "She's wonderful, Bathsheba. Everything I ever admired in a woman, and she doesn't even mind my lost arm."

"Danny," she said blankly.

"I will never abandon you," he added forcefully. "I'm going to complete the job as planned, and she's going to pay as planned. But the money is for you. Catherine and

I . . . We've discussed marriage. I can never repay you for how you cared for me after the war, but now you won't be stuck keeping house for me—"

"You rogue!" She jumped up and ran to throw her arms around him. "You're in love! Why wouldn't you tell me?"

He grinned bashfully. "Because I wanted to have the money first, and I refuse to take it from Catherine before the work is done. You would be welcome to live with us, of course, but"—he gave her a knowing look—"I suspect you might not wish to. With this sum, you should be able to keep this house and Mary. Catherine's manor house is in a quiet part of Greenwich, and it might be too remote for your taste."

She thought of Liam's secluded house and how lovely and private it was there. If she were newly married, a spinster sister-in-law was the last person she would want to share that house with. "Of course you want your own home, with your bride. When shall I meet her?"

"Soon," said her brother, his face brightening with relief and pride. "I've been trying to work out how to tell you for some time. Catherine—She advised me weeks ago that I ought to tell you."

Just as Liam had advised her to tell Danny, and have a life of her own. And now—oh goodness—she didn't need to decide about *Lady X*. She could tell Danny or not, and either way she would be independent.

She forced her mind away from that and back to her brother's happiness. She asked him about his betrothed bride, and to her amusement, Danny spoke at great and rhapsodic length about Catherine Brown. In his telling, she was beautiful, sensible, and utterly charming. Her late husband, a man twenty years her senior, had left her a comfortable income and a small manor near Greenwich.

Danny, who had once been a bit of a hell-raiser, was looking forward to life as a country gentleman.

When Danny had finished extolling his beloved's virtues, he gave Bathsheba a somewhat abashed look. "I could have mentioned her sooner, I suppose."

"You suppose rightly," she replied. "But I can see you're in love, so I must forgive you. No man is sensible when he's in love."

He ducked his head, grinning like a fool. "I should have known you'd take it well."

Bathsheba blinked in surprise. "You thought I wouldn't? Why?"

A flush covered her brother's face. He opened his mouth, then closed it without speaking. "Well—er—I meant to say . . ."

Suddenly she felt very conscious of the reticule on the chair beside her, the one she'd left at her lover's house after their last rendezvous. Danny hadn't told her because he worried that she would feel alone and unwanted, when all this time she'd been keeping her romantic activities from him, just as he had done with his. "Never mind," she said in a rush. "I understand."

"Perhaps you should come live with us," Danny replied, his face still pink. "I hate to think of you alone—"

"Don't be ridiculous." She steadfastly refused to look at the reticule. It seemed to be taunting her over her declaration to Liam that everything between them was over. If only she'd waited another day. If only Danny had told her this sooner. "Think of your Catherine, who will likely not want to share her home with her new husband's spinster sister."

He looked torn, but let it go. "I feel responsible for you, Bathsheba."

She forced an uncomfortable smile. "You shouldn't."

"I do. Our father would expect no less of me. If ever you are lonely or in need—"

"I'll be fine," she cut in forcefully, trying to fend off the image of sitting alone in this house, writing stories about love and passion, but never finding them. If she listened to the men around her, she'd end up sunk in pity over her sad state, and Bathsheba had a mortal disdain for self-pity. "Perfectly fine. Invite me to dine with you from time to time, provide a nephew or a niece for me to dote upon, and I shall be content."

His face eased. "Of course. Nothing daunts you! You've got more backbone than most men of my acquaintance, Bathsheba."

"As a woman," she said dryly, "I expect that's fairly typical."

He laughed. "No doubt." He rose. "I'm glad to have told you at last. It's been weighing on me for a while now."

"Then why didn't you say something sooner?" She shook her head. "What puzzling creatures men are."

He merely laughed again and went up the stairs. Bathsheba remained where she was, feeling at once happy and a little maudlin. Danny, married! She would have a new sister. Bathsheba said a heartfelt prayer that she and Catherine Brown took a liking to each other.

And now she wouldn't have to hide anything—not her writing, not her evening activities. She could even bring a lover here if she wished. Her gaze fell on the sofa where Liam had sat just half an hour previously, and her hand settled on the reticule he had returned. She hadn't even missed it, which was unusual for her. Bathsheba liked everything in its proper place.

Absently she pulled open the strings and drew out the

small notebook, and felt another pang in her heart. What a ninny Liam must have thought her that first night, planning to take notes when he was planning to drive her out of her mind with passion. On impulse she flipped through the pages of the notebook; what had she written in here?

At first she thought it was nothing of import; there were scribblings about her book, but she'd already written those parts. But halfway through there was a different handwriting, and she blushed as she realized it was Liam's.

He'd read her notes. He'd commented on them, too. Her mouth curved as she read his suggestions about the blacksmith; she'd made that character a clever fellow, just as Liam thought she ought to do. Some of his comments were so irreverent, she could almost see the sly expression on his face, which made her smile widen wistfully.

She turned another page, and her amusement slid away. There had been so much she wanted to know about seduction and pleasure. When Liam agreed to her daring proposal, she'd wanted to be prepared. She'd made a list and written down her questions.

And Liam had answered them.

In her notebook.

Chapter Twelve

Liam stalked down Totman Street in a terrible mood. He had pondered long and hard about what he ought to say to Bathsheba, but somehow he'd still made a hash of it. This was not what he had expected; normally his coolly rational approach achieved what he set out to do. Knowing Bathsheba as he did, he'd even though it would be best.

Did she really cling to secrecy because of her brother? It was hard to believe that. Daniel wasn't likely to throw her out, not after the way Bathsheba had saved his life and business. And Bathsheba herself wasn't cowed by much; she was eminently logical, unlike every other woman of Liam's acquaintance. On the other hand, Liam's interactions with Angus forced him to acknowledge that sibling relations were not always founded in logic and sense.

What was he to do now? Every day of the past three weeks had made the truth of Angus's words evident: This could only end well if she married him. And he'd botched it.

He hadn't made the decision to go see her lightly. It had been over three weeks since she spent the night with him in St. John's Wood, her soft warm body curled up next to his. Three weeks was more than enough time to realize what he wanted and formulate a cogent argument that would persuade her. He'd thought she would be receptive; there had been that moment when she threw her arms around his neck and kissed him, for all the world as if she cared about him. That moment, Liam now recognized, had been his chance to tell her he hadn't thought about that damned bargain in weeks, that he could only think of her and how much he wanted her.

But then his brother appeared and ruined the moment. Caught off guard, Liam had done the wrong thing, which was to send Bathsheba away and let Angus stay. More than once he had replayed the scene in his mind, wherein he ordered Angus away and swept Bathsheba back inside the house to explain at length why their affair ought to continue indefinitely, with a wedding thrown in for good measure.

So much for his plan to work gradually toward telling her he loved her. How could he be so decisive and bold in business, but second-guess every word when it came to a woman?

He reached Tottenham Court Road and scowled at the heavy traffic that blocked his way. He must regroup and try again. What would persuade her? He couldn't get their conversation out of his mind, in the dark before dawn as she lay in his arms. She was clever and resilient and strong. In the face of heartbreak and trouble she had held herself together, caring for her brother and fighting to keep their business going. Liam admired all that tremendously, and yet it meant he had less to offer her. In fact, the only thing he had to offer . . .

Was the one thing she had asked of him. Passion.

Abruptly he spun on his heel, almost colliding with a plump matron behind him. He said a hasty apology as she squawked in protest, but his steps didn't pause as he strode back the way he'd come.

He rapped loudly on the door of her house. It hadn't been half an hour since he'd left, she must be still at home. When the wide-eyed maid opened the door, he pushed past her into the tiny hall. "Is Miss Crawford—?"

She appeared in the parlor doorway before he could even finish the question. Without hesitation he closed the distance in two steps and caught her in his arms as he kissed her, desperately, hungrily, longingly. She gave a startled squeak, but then her arms went around his neck and she kissed him back. Her mouth was soft and willing, and Liam promptly forgot everything else.

When he lifted his head, she blinked up at him as if dazed. "What—?"

"That's what I meant to do before," he said. Belatedly realizing the maid was standing behind him, watching avidly, he pulled Bathsheba back into the parlor and shut the door.

Her blush was beautiful. In fact, *she* was beautiful, her hair disarranged, her eyes soft, her mouth rosy from his kiss. Liam couldn't think how he'd never seen it before.

"But you said . . ."

"That was my mistake. I spoke when I should have acted."

She blushed deeper, but without any sign of disapproval. His confidence returned in full force. Now that he had her in his arms, everything felt right again. "We're good together, you and I," he said, cupping her cheek in one hand. "Always have been. Always will be, I suspect."

"Liam," she said, her face scarlet. "I . . . I . . ." With a great effort, she seemed to gather herself, pushing back a little and finally meeting his eyes. "You wrote in my book."

He'd stared at those pages in her little book for hours. "I couldn't help but notice it was full of unanswered questions."

Her face grew very still. "And you decided to answer them."

"Yes." How had he never noticed the tiny cleft in her determined chin? It was entrancing.

"Did you mean what you wrote?"

She'd read it. Even more, he belatedly realized it was clutched in her hand. His heart began a hard thudding in his chest, and a smile slowly curved his lips. He didn't need to think of what to say; he'd already expressed himself. He plucked the book from her fingers. "Let me see . . ." He flipped through to the first page, titled *Seduction*. "Seduction is the art of making a woman fall in love with you, to bare her heart, to see her soul, to know her so deeply and intimately you would happily lose yourself in her and never want to be found. The seduction has succeeded when she wishes to do the same to you. It is the deepest sort of intimacy to bare one's physical form as well as one's heart to a lover, and there is also much pleasure to be gained in the removal of clothing by both."

She was watching him, her eyes wary. He nodded. "All true."

He turned the page to *Timing*. "Lovemaking should last until both have found their ultimate pleasure, whether this be accomplished at languorous length or in vigorously short order. After a lengthy separation, a man may hunger for his lover so desperately he would endure any inconvenience, risk any chance of scandal or condemnation, at one inviting glance from her. In other cases, it may better please both lovers to draw out the pleasure for hours. Sating this hunger in a variety of locales, and employing a variety of positions, will never fail to inspire a thrill of delight and prevent any trace of boredom. It is a firm fact, universally acknowledged, that any opportunity to please his lover, in any way he may, will be eagerly seized by a man caught in the coils of love."

"The coils of love," she whispered.

"It's a very serious condition." He turned another page and read what he'd written under *Location*. "There is no place on earth I would not want to make love to you."

"Truly?"

"Can you doubt it?"

She hesitated, her eyes shadowed. Liam cast off all subtlety. "I want you," he said. "I want you in my bed every night, with no thought of scurrying away in the morning."

"Only because of the lo-lovemaking?" Color rose in her cheeks as she stumbled over the last word.

Gently he tapped the notebook. "You must not have read all." He turned to the last page, the one he had written only that morning before he went to Totman Street, the answer to her question about kisses.

"A kiss is the communion of one soul with another," he read. "A sharing of breath, of life, of love. At first I thought you would not welcome it; you only wanted knowledge, you said. I believed you did not love me, nor want to love me, so I avoided it. I did not want to fall in love with you, so I resisted.

"But I am helpless to change my own feelings, and finally I could not escape what I wanted most: to feel you were mine, as I have felt myself to be yours since the moment you removed your cloak and wore almost nothing underneath." Her eyes were wide with wonder. Liam dropped the book to the floor; he didn't need to read the rest, for he knew it by heart. "You are like no other woman

I've ever known. You are honorable, clever, sensible, and devoted, and since our affair began I have realized you are even more: passionate, wicked, and lovely . . ." She jerked in his arms, amazed, and he nodded once. "If you want nothing else from me, I will treasure the memory of our three nights together, and vow on my honor to keep them a secret between us, but you should know that I want more—your passion, your intelligence, your love."

There was a long moment of silence. Bathsheba seemed struck dumb. Liam realized he was holding his breath, waiting for her response.

Her head came up. "Why didn't you say any of this before?"

"It took me awhile to find the words."

"Are you certain you mean them?" He scowled, and she blushed. "That is . . ."

"Yes. Every word."

"But what about—"

"Bathsheba," he interrupted, out of patience and burning to know, "will you marry me?"

She gave a quick laugh, startled. "Of course I will. I've been in love with you for ages. Why do you think I asked you to seduce me?"

That brought him up short. "That was the reason?"

Bathsheba lowered her eyes. "You thought it was because you're so very handsome and have the devil's own charm, didn't you?"

He grinned. She'd said yes. *Of course I will.* No doubt or hesitation. And she was in love with him. "Naturally. And also . . . Because I wouldn't think you immoral for asking."

"That would be hypocritical," she pointed out—his lovely, logical Bathsheba. "But I had to know if you truly meant what you wrote."

Liam tipped up her face. "Is that any way to proclaim your deep and unwavering love for a man? By questioning his honesty?"

"I only wanted to hear you say it!"

"I love you," he breathed, his mouth brushing hers. "Are you satisfied now?"

She blushed, and smiled, and opened her mouth to reply just as the door behind them burst open.

"MacGregor," exclaimed Daniel Crawford. "What the devil?"

Liam looked around. Bathsheba's brother stood in the doorway, a fierce frown on his face. "I'm here to see your sister—"

"I'm not certain I should allow that," returned Crawford. "Let her go."

"Because I want to marry her," Liam finished. "You're ruining my proposal."

The other man's jaw sagged. "Bathsheba," he said in a tone of blank shock. "You? And this rogue?" Before either could speak, he said again, "Let her go, damn you. How long has this been going on?"

Liam let his arm fall, but Bathsheba didn't step away. If anything she pressed closer, her palm on his chest, over his heart. "You're a fine one to complain, Daniel Crawford," she told her brother. "Not saying a word about Mrs. Brown until you were betrothed to her!" She looked up at Liam. "He's marrying a widow from Greenwich. He told me she hired him to rebind her library—"

"What? No, she did!" protested Crawford.

"Just this morning he confided that he's marrying her. He won't need me to look after him anymore, though goodness knows, I hope Mrs. Brown understands what she's getting into with him—" She broke off and shook her head, looking stern.

Liam had to bite back a laugh at the expression on the other man's face as his sister dressed him down. "Felicitations, Crawford."

Daniel was no fool; he knew when he was routed. His posture eased, but his frown lingered. "I suppose you've accepted him, Bathsheba?"

"I didn't have a chance, before you burst in without invitation," she said. She turned to Liam. "Yes, Mr. MacGregor, I accept your offer of marriage." As if it were a business proposal they had negotiated.

"I'm delighted to hear it, Miss Crawford," he replied politely, and then he kissed her, not caring what Crawford thought. Dimly he heard the sound of the door, and when he finally raised his head to smile into Bathsheba's flushed, glowing face, they were alone. "This is not a business arrangement," he told her.

"No?" She beamed at him. "What sort is it?"

"Obviously marital; possibly including children, who, I expect, will require your keen oversight if they take after me. But primarily . . ." He slid one hand around her nape as she gave a little laugh. "Primarily it's one of love and passion."

"That is the only sort of arrangement I want," she whispered, and he kissed her again to seal the bargain. Not once, but several times.

The Scandals Series

Don't miss a single scandalous moment . . .
THE SECRET OF MY SEDUCTION is only the ending.

LOVE AND OTHER SCANDALS
Tristan, Lord Burke isn't a marrying man—until a droll, sharp-witted wallflower starts haunting his dreams.

IT TAKES A SCANDAL
Sebastian Vane is an outcast, unfit to marry an heiress. But true love is no match for even the darkest scandal.

ALL'S FAIR IN LOVE AND SCANDAL
Douglas Bennet, notorious rake, makes a scandalous wager—which may cost him his heart.

LOVE IN THE TIME OF SCANDAL
Benedict Lennox, Lord Atherton, needs a wife—but the most likely bride is everything he never knew he wanted in a woman.

A STUDY IN SCANDAL
Lord George Churchill-Gray is an artist, not a knight in shining armor—until a runaway heiress tumbles into his arms.

SIX DEGREES OF SCANDAL
James Weston is determined to save the woman he loves—but lost—from a villain . . . and win her back in the process.

About the Author

Caroline Linden was born a reader, not a writer. She earned a math degree from Harvard University and wrote computer software before turning to fiction. Since then, her books have been translated into seventeen languages, and won the NEC-RWA Reader's Choice Award, the Daphne du Maurier Award, the NJRW Golden Leaf Award, and RWA's RITA Award.

Visit her at *www.carolinelinden.com* to join her VIP readers' list for an exclusive short story, sneak peeks at upcoming titles, behind-the-scenes looks, and to get notified when she has new books out.